Whisper Goodbye

Whisper Goodbye

by

Dorothy Nafus Morrison

Troll Associates

A TROLL BOOK, published by Troll Associates,
Mahwah, NJ 07430

Published by arrangement with Atheneum Publishers, a subsidiary of Macmillan, Inc. For information address Atheneum Publishers, Macmillan, Inc., 866 Third Avenue, New York, New York 10022.

First Troll Printing, 1987

Printed in the United States of America

10 9 8 7 6 5 4 3 2 1

ISBN 0-8167-1045-7

with love
to Anne and Jenny
who introduced me
to the real
Whisper Please

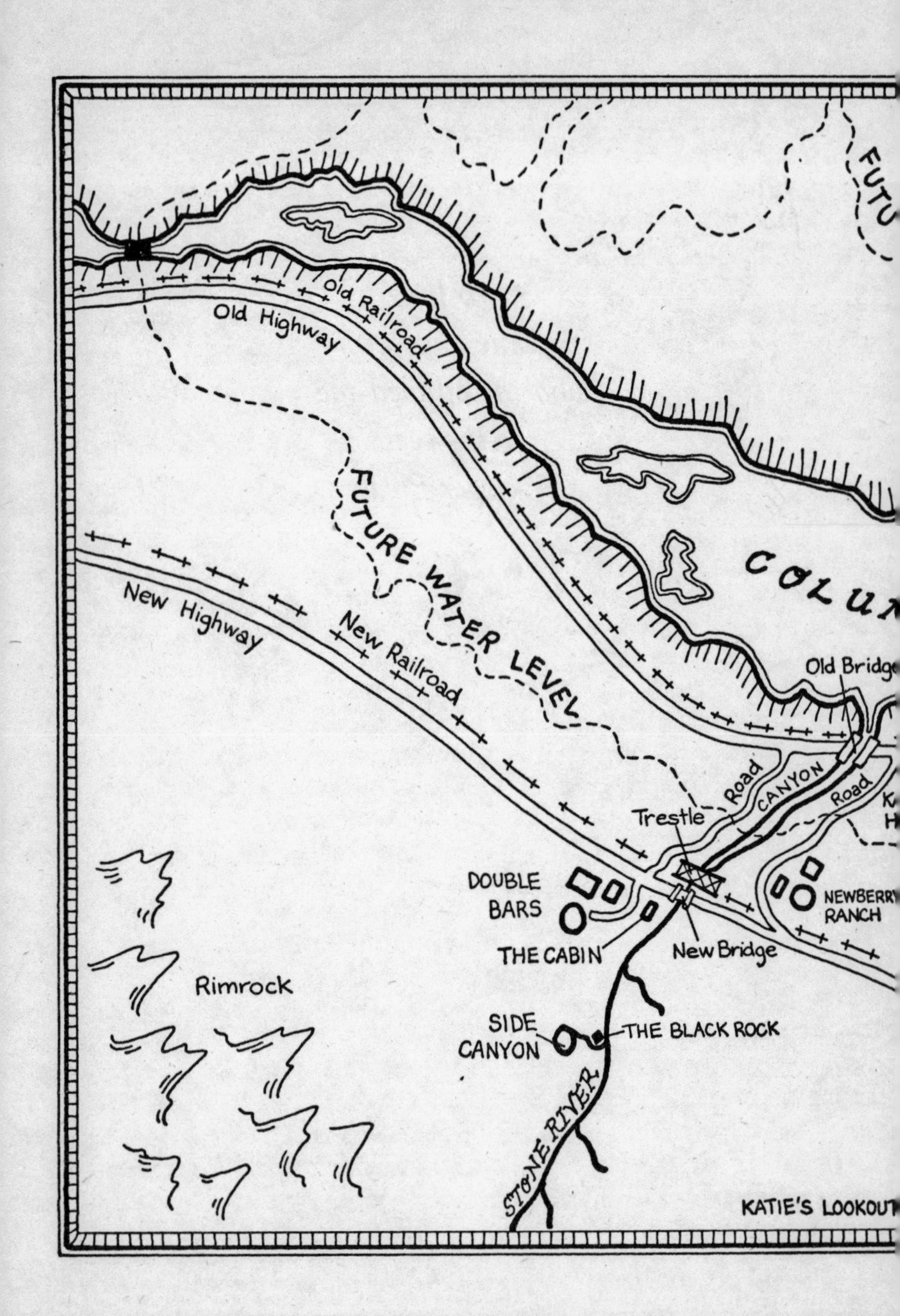

Old Railroad
Old Highway
FUTURE WATER LEVEL
New Highway
New Railroad
Old Bridg
Road
CANYON
Road
Trestle
DOUBLE BARS
THE CABIN
New Bridge
NEWBERRY RANCH
Rimrock
SIDE CANYON
THE BLACK ROCK
STONE RIVER
KATIE'S LOOKOUT

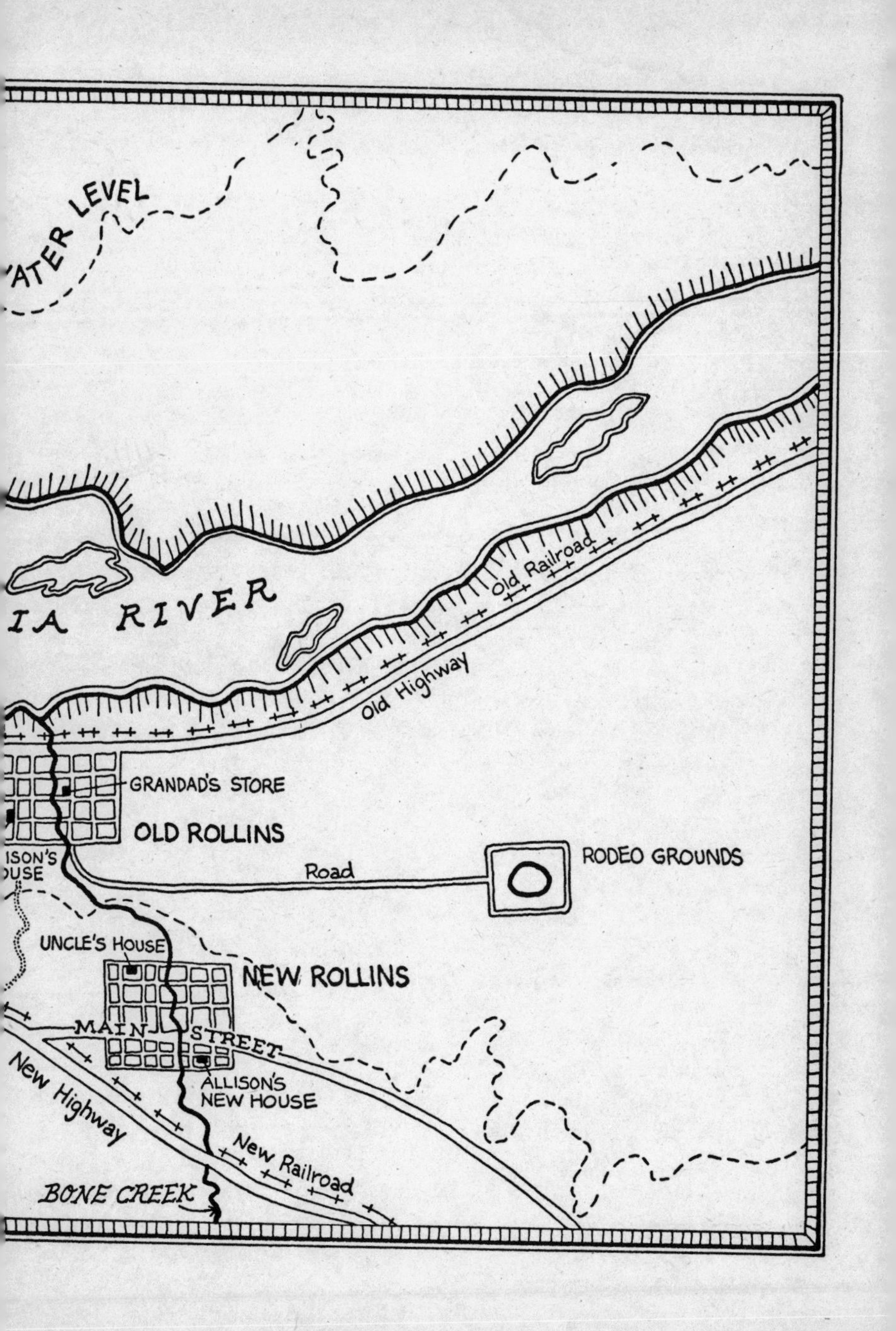
ATER LEVEL
IA RIVER
Old Railroad
Old Highway
GRANDAD'S STORE
OLD ROLLINS
LISON'S
OUSE
Road
RODEO GROUNDS
UNCLE'S HOUSE
NEW ROLLINS
MAIN STREET
ALLISON'S
NEW HOUSE
New Highway
New Railroad
BONE CREEK

Contents

1 *Can It Be True?* 3
2 *Rodeo* 11
3 *Grandad's Plan* 21
4 *The Girl with the Yellow Kitten* 30
5 *Lookout Rock* 43
6 *Stone Canyon* 54
7 *Aunt Harriet and the Double Bar S* 67
8 *The Last Homecoming* 82
9 *Searching* 94
10 *Old House, Old Town* 107
11 *The Crazy Eight* 119
12 *Allison* 129
13 *The Last Day of Business* 139
14 *The Trestle* 146
15 *Time of Decision* 157
16 *Lake Rollins* 170

AUTHOR'S NOTE 181

1

Can It Be True?

Katie McNeill was running. Her sneakers thudded on the cement walk, and her light-brown hair flopped around her shoulders, as she raced on and on, under the cottonwood trees. Downhill she ran. Downhill—downhill—toward the center of town. She had to get to Brad and find out what was wrong. He knew a lot about Grandad's affairs. He'd know whether it was true, what Michelle had said.

It can't be true, Katie told herself, as she pounded along. *Michelle is only a little kid, and she's got things all mixed up. But still*—the thought wouldn't go away—*Michelle's grandmother said so. She's Gram's best friend. And something's been going on all week.*

Small for thirteen years, slim, agile, Katie was

growing hot. Her flannel shirt encased her like a bandage, and the hair at the edge of her cowboy hat felt pasted down. She stopped once, to get a better grip on the boots and lunch box she was carrying, then ran on again.

It's all right, perfectly all right, she assured herself. She wouldn't wonder why Grandad had left so suddenly on this busiest of all weekends. She wouldn't think of the times she'd walked into a room, and he and Gram stopped talking, then began again all in a rush. She wouldn't think of last night, when she'd been too excited to sleep and had heard their voices downstairs rustling on and on, while the tall clock chimed away the quarter-hours.

By the time Katie reached the treeless parking lot of the Congregational church, she was out of breath, so she slowed to a walk and glanced up at the hills that almost surrounded the town: smooth, treeless, dotted with sagebrush, and dark now with the burned-dry brown of early fall. It was early September, rodeo weekend, the most super-special weekend of the whole year. Katie caught her breath. In an hour, or maybe a little more, she'd be riding Whisper in the very first barrel race of her entire life.

Her older cousin Brad, who had helped with the training, had at last decided it was time to try. "But don't expect much, Kate," he had warned. "Whisper's green yet, and you are, too. You'll be there just for experience. Understand?"

"I'll remember," she had joyfully promised. They had paid off, all those hot summer days on Uncle Steve's ranch, working with Whisper and helping out wherever she could. Not that she'd minded. Even mucking out a stall was fun—well, almost fun—when she could ride afterward.

But now, was everything going to be spoiled?

Breathing more easily, Katie began to run again and emerged into Main Street of Rollins, a dry little dusty town in the ranch country of eastern Oregon. Although the street was only a few blocks long, it was wide, with rocky, jagged Bone Creek Ravine snaking its way right down the middle, bordered by a row of slender poplar trees. It reminded Katie of boulevards on TV travel shows, except Bone Creek had an auto bridge at each intersection, and lots of wooden footbridges.

With a final burst of speed she *clop-clopped* across one of these and came to Grandad's drugstore. Now at last she would see Brad and find out—at least try to find out—what he knew. She bounded up the three concrete steps and flung open the door with its jingling bell.

Katie had loved the drugstore ever since she first came to live with Grandad and Gram, more than six years ago, after the boating accident that had taken her parents' lives. It was small, but clean and bright, with a white pharmacy at the back, a black pot-bellied stove that managed to look both jolly and inconvenient, and hanging lights of many-colored glass.

Behind the chrome soda fountain stood Brad, Uncle Steve's son, who was a senior in high school. Tall and lanky, with wavy, light-brown hair and a broad grin, he was washing dishes and whistling, with a white towel tied around his waist and soapsuds almost to his elbows. Brad never did anything by halves.

When Katie burst through the door, he wiped his hands on the towel. "Well! Special delivery?"

She wrinkled her nose. "Sustenance," she said, handing over the lunch box. "So you won't eat up all the profits."

"Thanks. Ice cream is great, but I've had so much already that my insides are frozen stiff." He unwrapped a sandwich and began to gulp it in huge bites, washing each one down with milk.

Katie hopped onto a wire-backed chair beside the counter and wound her feet around its legs. "Busy today?" she asked.

"M-m-mp," Brad mumbled through a sandwich. In a moment he said, "They just about ran me ragged at the fountain for a while, until everybody went to the fair grounds. Had some prescriptions I couldn't fill by myself." He poured a glass of milk. "Any word from Grandad? Did he call?"

"Not yet. Gram thinks he'll be back for dinner." Katie leaned forward and gripped the edge of the counter. "Brad, something happened. On my way here I passed the Sanders house, and Michelle was out in her swing."

"Michelle? Oh, sure. I know her. Stringy little kid."

"Yes. Well, she always wants to talk about Whisper, so I stopped for a minute. And she said her mother thinks it's funny Grandad has gone away just now, and that maybe it's because a big store is coming. Could it be a chain?"

"It not only could be, it is. Sav-U-Mor. The word just got out."

"Then Michelle was at least partly right. Brad, she told me something else. Something *awful*—that her mother said such a big store would be hard on Grandad, and she hoped I wouldn't have to sell Whisper." Katie's voice dropped to a frightened murmur. "Brad . . . *sell Whisper!* Has he told you anything about that?"

"Michelle's only a kid—four years old, maybe? Five?"

"She's almost six. I think she gets things pretty straight."

"But her parents might not. People make lots of wild guesses. You know that." Brad opened another carton of milk.

"Has Grandad said anything about selling Whisper?"

"Not to me."

"Something's going on," Katie insisted. "Why

did Grandad leave the store on rodeo weekend, when we're so busy? Do you know where he went?"

Brad moved slowly, straightening the edges of his sandwich with unnecessary care. "Your guess is as good as mine."

"You know something about it! I can tell!" Katie's voice was growing shrill, for it frightened her to have Brad so careful and slow. "Grandad is gone, and Gram's knitting like mad, with her lips buttoned tight. She always knits when she's bothered. I didn't dare even ask her what's going on."

Brad seemed to be concentrating on his milk.

"Is it something about the dam?" For an instant Katie visualized the huge structure that was being built just downstream on the Columbia River, one that would flood the entire area and force the whole town of Rollins to move to higher ground. Grandad, like everyone else, was building high up on the hills. "Or something about our new house? Or store?" Katie persisted.

At this Brad grinned. "Watch out, Kate—you'll boil over." Then, more seriously, he added, "Suppose Grandad told me something, or suppose I'd guessed. Would it be right for me to pass it on?" Opening a plastic box that held an oversize piece of cherry pie, he whistled. "Another of your culinary masterpieces?"

"Not this time. Gram made it, except I rolled the crust." Katie handed him a paper napkin from the chrome container on the counter. "So you really do know something or you've guessed! Something bad!" she exclaimed. "Tell me, and when Grandad springs it, I'll act as surprised as can be."

Brad shook his head. "Katie, I don't know much of anything, and it isn't about your horse, and it's for him to tell, not me." He began to devour the pie.

"Bradley Edward McNeill!" Katie slid off the chair, landing with a thump. "Don't you care about anything except that pie? Doesn't it matter to you that Grandad's gone away? That the dam is going to drown his store and our house, and he has to build new ones? That we're losing our town?"

Brad was wholly serious now. "Sure it matters," he said. "But, Kate . . . we aren't really going to lose the town. Just move it up onto the hills, and who knows. . . . We'll have a lake, a big one, which may be a good thing. Navigation will pick up, and recreational boating, too. It'll put Rollins on the map."

"I don't want it on the map. I like it just the way it is." Katie glared at her tall cousin. "It's easy for you to keep cool, because you don't really care. You'll be in college and won't have to live in the horrid, shiny new town." She drew a deep breath. "I have to go," she said, for if Brad didn't understand, she couldn't possibly explain. "The barrel race comes early. I hope Whisper isn't too scared. She isn't used to noise."

"Dave'll keep her calm," Brad replied, referring to the middle-aged cowboy who worked part-time on Uncle Steve's ranch, and who was taking care of Whisper today. "Be sure you cool her down afterwards."

"I won't forget. 'Bye." In one quick movement Katie scooped up her riding boots and started toward the door.

Outside, she paused for a moment on the steps to gaze at the boxy little stores, then up and up toward the homes that were being built high on the hills. It was hard to believe that the Columbia River, which was just a silver shine at the far end of Bone Creek Ravine, could rise to there.

How will Rollins look when it's all a lake? she wondered. Could you ride out in a boat and look down, and see trees waving their branches under the water? Would you see fish swimming, right where those swallows were flying now? She caught her breath. Would fish go swimming in and out the windows of Grandad's drugstore?

There, she thought, looking up again, *away up there is our own new house. We can stand on its deck and watch the water come in. We can see it creeping up and up, lapping at the doors down here, lapping at the windows, closing over the roofs. And then, instead of a town, we'll see a lake.*

This will be the second time my whole life has been torn to pieces. And if Grandad is having trouble. . . .

Soberly, she started up the hill.

2

Rodeo

"Jeff Chambers! Riding Blue Blazer!" As Katie neared the rodeo grounds, she heard the booming loudspeaker. "He's over! Easing down! Working his right hand into that hand-hold. *There he goes!*"

Jeff, that's Linda's brother, thought Katie. They're riding broncs now. I hope Jeff drew a good one. Hot as she was after the long uphill hike, she walked a little faster, past the parking lot and through the gate.

Inside, the bleachers were nearly full, and people were sitting on blankets on the opposite slope. Shrieking with excitement, children slid down the bank, or ran back and forth with billows of pink cotton candy, while the loudspeaker blared, horses whinnied, and cattle bawled. Over it all hung a rich mixed smell of hot dogs and popcorn, animals and dust.

Katie soon found Whisper tied up behind the chutes. As a foal she had been a dappled steel gray, but year by year her coat had become lighter, until now it was palest silver, with faint circles on her flanks, almost invisible—like watered silk. Even here, the quietest part of the grounds, she was frightened, and quivered as Katie stroked her forehead.

"Yes, I've brought you a carrot," she said. "But you have to race first. If I feed you now, you'll think you're all through, and you won't try."

"Whuff-ff," said Whisper, with her special snuffle.

How many carrots had she given Whisper, Katie wondered, since the first time she had seen her as a day-old foal, slim and wobbly, all legs and big dark eyes, standing beside her mother in the roomy box stall?

"She's yours, if you want her," Uncle Steve had said. He was a lawyer, the only one in Rollins, but he lived just outside of town on the remnants of the Double Bar S Ranch and raised a few horses for a hobby.

"*Oh!*" Katie had been too astonished to say more.

"You'll have to find a name," Uncle Steve had said. "Think hard, now."

The foal had no marks—star, spots, white stockings—to help in the choice. She was just an all-over dappled gray, with a quick little whisk of tail and bristly gray mane. Katie had concentrated for days, trying to think of something splendid enough. But she noticed the special nicker, a soft, breathy, friendly snuffle.

"Like a whisper!" Katie had said. "Can we name her that, Uncle Steve? Whisper? Please?" In her excitement she was jumping up and down.

"Whisper Please? That's just right!" he had agreed.

So Katie's foal was named Whisper Please, although they called her Whisper for short. And now, three years later, she was ready for her first race.

As Katie hurried through the outer arena, her stomach lurched and her knees felt like strands of rope. She spotted Dave sitting on a wooden box. "There's your gear," he said, pointing toward a fence, its rails festooned with saddles, worn or new, black, brown, tan.

Before claiming her own, Katie sat down on an overturned bucket to change her sneakers for riding boots. I *can't* have outgrown them already, she thought, as she tugged the first one over her heel. It pinched; her toes rubbed. But she jammed them on, then jumped up and checked Whisper's hooves for stones. As she expected, Dave had done a good job.

"We're almost ready, girl," she murmured, pulling her horse's head down so she could plant a kiss on its forehead. She heaved the saddle off the fence and flipped it into place, cinching it tight—and tighter—and tighter still, then mounted and walked Whisper toward a group of barrel racers at the end of the staging area.

Here, so close to the arena, the shouts of the crowd frightened Whisper, who began to step sidewise and toss her head. "Steady there, steady. It's all right," Katie said in her most soothing voice, although her own stomach was doing flip-flops.

Because this was a teen-age race, most of the riders were in high school, and she was overjoyed to see one of her eighth-grade classmates, Linda Chambers. Round-faced, with thick blond bangs, Linda was riding a slender brown mare, and behind her, like a miniature procession, came her two little sisters, one on a medium-size spotted pony, the other on a black Shetland.

"Linda!" exclaimed Katie. "I'm *so* glad you're here! I'm scared nearly to pieces, and Whisper is, too. She's really hyper." As another horse passed, Whisper snorted and tried to circle. "But I thought you were all through racing."

"I am. I just came for fun, along with my gang here." Linda's braces shone as she grinned at her little sisters. "I tried—you know that—because my dad loves rodeos so much, but just thinking about it ties my stomach in knots." Linda ran her fingers through her horse's mane. "Good old Nutmeg. I love you. I just don't like to race."

"I know." For a moment Katie visualized Linda's room on the Rocking C Ranch, its shelves heaped with movie magazines, and walls all but hidden by pictures of actresses. Linda—round, cheerful Linda—took voice lessons and dancing lessons and longed to be slinky and mysterious. But she was so much fun, just the way she was, lots better than being a siren, Katie thought.

Just then Mary Anne Hennessey, a high school junior, rode close beside Whisper, who snorted and shook her head. "It's your first race, isn't it?" asked Mary Anne, sitting tall on her big sorrel gelding Scooter. "That's the hardest one. I'll never forget Scooter's first. He didn't just graze a barrel, he ran right into one." She laughed, while Whisper made another circle. "Hold her steadier," Mary Anne advised. "Hang on tight. Be tough, so she can't keep turning her head. The more she looks around, the more scared she'll be."

"I'll try," said Katie, wishing she had long legs like Mary Anne's. However, as soon as she tightened her knees and reins, Whisper quieted down. "Thanks, Mary Anne," Katie said. "I guess I have a lot to learn."

"You're doing fine. The only way to start is to start. Every race gets easier."

To Katie, the next half-hour seemed to last forever. She rode Whisper around the outer yard, chatted with Linda, consoled Jeff, who had been thrown. Three times she dismounted to check Whisper's blanket and cinch straps. She shortened her stirrups, lengthened them, shortened them again. Fought down the loop-the-loops in her stomach. When at last it was time for her race, she rode to the edge of the arena with about a dozen other girls.

The barrels were in place, three white-painted oil drums, set in a triangle. *They're too close*, thought Katie, for a few panicky seconds. *A hundred times too close. I can't make such sharp turns*. But she knew the distances had been carefully measured.

Mentally she ran the course. Past the starting flag. Clockwise around the first barrel. Across the arena. Counterclockwise around the next. If only Whisper took that one neatly! She hated that first counterclockwise turn. And then to the end barrel, counterclockwise around, and streak for home.

"Remember it all, girl," murmured Katie, stroking the bristly hairs on Whisper's neck. "You know how it's done."

The first three riders raced and returned. One from the other side of the Columbia River, on a palomino called Honey Bear, clocked eighteen and nine-tenths seconds, but was penalized five for knocking over a barrel. The next two were barely average.

And then Katie heard the loud speaker. "Katie McNeill! Riding Whisper Please." It boomed. It echoed. It seemed to pound its way through her whole body, and her heart sank right into her boots.

"Here we go, girl!" she exclaimed, as she rode to the starting point. Whisper pricked forward her ears.

"At 'em!" Katie leaned forward over the shiny neck. Dug in her heels. Relaxed the reins. And Whisper ran.

Clockwise around the first barrel, with no mishaps and a good, tight turn. Across to the second and counterclockwise. Katie tightened her knees, grabbed the gray mane, leaned farther forward, crooned in the horse's ear, "Around . . . around . . . take it close, now! Good girl!" She swerved like a veteran. To the end for the final turn, so swift that Katie lost her hat. And then, with hair streaming and Whisper's hooves pounding, she dashed across the line.

"Nineteen point three seconds!" bellowed the speaker, while the grimy cowboy who brought her the fallen hat grinned and said, "Good run." Whisper was in the lead.

She held it for the next rider—the next—and another. But Mary Anne, the very last one, leaned her body forward and gave Scooter one sharp lick with the whip. Putting it between her teeth, she seized his mane with her left hand, while her right laid the reins toward one side and then the other—around a barrel . . . and around . . . and around. A sizzling race, Katie knew. Clean and sure, on a truly exciting horse. She held her breath when the announcement began.

"Eighteen point five!"

Katie gulped. For a few moments she had actually thought she was going to win, and now that she'd lost by less than a second her throat grew tight and her lips began to tremble. What had Brad told her?

You're in it just for the experience. He was right, of course, only it was hard to come so close, and miss.

And then she saw a cowboy, a stranger, not even young and glamorous, but just a battered, dusty cowboy with blood on his face, carrying his hat, limping and grinning. He reminded her of the hundreds she had watched, who rode their best but took their losses with courage and good humor. At least she had won something, which was lots better than she'd expected for her very first race.

"You're wonderful, just wonderful!" she told Whisper, as she patted the warm gray neck. Tilting her hat back on her head, she sat up straight in the saddle and rode to Mary Anne. "Neat race," she called out, smiling. "Scooter's a super horse, and you rode him just right."

"Whisper is good, too," said Mary Anne, flushed and sparkling. "With another year or so she's going to be a real winner."

"I hope so. I'm going to really work at it," Katie replied. Her heart beat fast as she rode into the winners' circle and received a large red rosette, which she fastened to Whisper's bridle.

In the outer area, she exchanged the saddle and bridle for a blanket and halter, walked the horse to cool her down, and gave her a drink from a blue plastic pail. Just as Whisper finished the last slobbery drops, Dave suddenly appeared, his face one big grin.

"I'll take her back to the ranch," he said. "Brad

should have seen you run that race. It was a dandy."

"I tried my best," Katie answered, as she handed over the lead rope. Thankfully she pulled off the too-tight boots and wiggled her toes.

Golden dust shimmered in the sun. The air smelled of new lumber, of hay, of horses and leather and sweaty saddle blankets. A wispy cloud glided overhead, cooling the arena, but in a moment it was gone, leaving everything again bright and hot. Katie drank a long, icy Coke as she eagerly followed every event—calf roping, bulldogging, team roping—for in each one she saw cowboys she knew. And still, in the back of her mind, was a nagging undercurrent of worry. Grandad's trip . . . the night-time conferences. Something was happening, she felt sure. Something she wouldn't like.

When the last calf was thrown, the last horse ridden, she started to walk home, hot, dusty, and unbelievably tired. On her way out of the arena she was stopped several times by people who had noticed Whisper's near-win.

One was Linda's father, a wiry, enthusiastic little man, immensely proud of his children and interested in their friends. "Splendid race," he called with a wave of his hand.

"Thank you," Katie called back.

He was supervising the complicated job of loading their animals into a large trailer, and as Katie walked on, she heard him say, "Easy—you're next.

Bring up Nutmeg now." Linda was there, too, and Jeff, and the little sisters, all helping as best they could.

Just before Katie left the fair grounds, another acquaintance, a Mr. Whittaker who lived on the huge Crazy Eight Ranch, overtook her. "I was proud of you today, Katie," he rumbled.

"Proud?" asked Katie, puzzled and a little awed, for he was one of the biggest men she had ever seen, with hulking shoulders and wintry blue eyes.

"That's right," he continued. "I've an extra interest in your little mare, because her dam is Lacey Lady, that I sold to your uncle, and her sire was mine, too. I like to see my stock turning out well."

"I remember now—Uncle Steve told me about it."

"Guess I did wrong, selling the line when I did," the big man continued. "She's got the form and speed of a good cow pony. Just the kind I like." He touched his hat and turned away.

As Katie walked down the hill, the dark cloud of worry returned. Why had Mr. Whittaker said that? Had he been hinting? Had he heard something about Grandad selling Whisper? Of course not, she stoutly told herself. He was just trying to be friendly. She wouldn't pay any attention to it.

She'd only think about the rodeo, and all the rodeos to come. Next year she would enter again and try harder, and neither she nor Whisper would be so green. Next year she'd have a better chance to win.

3

Grandad's Plan

Going home was quick, for it was downhill nearly all the way. Just as Katie rounded the last corner, she saw the shutters standing open on the house next door, where her best friend Judy used to live. The people who rented it must have moved in, she thought, slowing down. But the next second she broke into a run, for Grandad's car was in the driveway. He had come back.

Her grandparents' house was well away from the street, at the end of a curved sidewalk, and it seemed to peer out from its overgrown, ancient shrubs. Katie loved its long porch, like a jaw, with posts for teeth, its jogs and angles—cupolas, dormers, bay windows. Most especially she loved the rounded tower on one corner, which was two stories tall and topped with a pointed roof like a rocket.

As she climbed the steep stairs to the porch, she glanced fondly at the door, with colored fan-shaped glass panes above and amber ones all down the sides. When she was little, she used to stand with her hands cupped around her eyes, gazing through the wavy glass. The dark woodwork inside, high narrow doorways, and winding stairs had been all squiggly, as if the house were under water. And it soon will be, she thought mournfully, turning the china doorknob.

In the front hall, a woolly little gray dog, like a dustmop on legs, raced in barking and scampered joyfully around her feet. "Hi, Tully." She gave him a quick pat, then hurried into the big, square kitchen, where Grandad was standing beside the stove and frying meat, while Gram gave him directions. "Turn it down a bit, it sounds too hot," she was saying.

Katie ran to her grandfather and flung her arms around his waist. "Grandad! You're back!"

"Safe and sound," he said, laying down his fork to return her hug. Although his hair and bristly eyebrows were white, he stood erect, and he was tall and spare. "How was the race?" he asked.

"Mary Anne won, with eighteen point five. But Whisper ran a good race and came in second. Nineteen point three. For a while I thought I'd won. I *wanted* to win, Grandad. You can't imagine how much. But still—it's my first race—and *look!*" She proudly showed them her red ribbon. "Whisper was wonderful."

"She's a good horse. But you trained her, don't forget that," said Grandad, again picking up the fork.

"Did you give Brad his lunch?" asked Gram as she sliced a tomato. She was sitting on a sofa by the window, with a pan of vegetables beside her and a bowl in her lap. A frail little white-haired lady with rosy cheeks and bright eyes, she knitted when she was troubled, worked crossword puzzles when she was calm, and in between she chatted with her elderly neighbors over endless cups of tea. Tonight she was humming as she made a salad, although her gnarled hands moved awkwardly.

"I delivered it, pie and all. And it was gone in nothing flat." Katie set her riding boots in the back entry.

When she returned to the kitchen, Grandad had turned over the meat and was pouring hot water into the teapot. "I stopped a minute at the store," he said. "Brad's been pretty busy."

"Cowboys really go for ice cream," Katie told him.

Tully bounced his ball and sat on his haunches, black eyes pleading through his fringe of hair. "Not now, Tully," she said, laughing. "I'll play with you later on." Plates clattered as she set them on the round table in the center of the room. Wouldn't Grandad *ever* tell what he'd been doing? Surely it was nothing serious, for he looked just the same as always: smiling, unhurried, wearing his old gray comfortable sweater. If he didn't explain pretty soon, she'd ask him straight out.

In a few minutes she put the hot dishes in place, while Grandad helped Gram. *Her foot's bad tonight*, thought Katie, noticing how slowly her grandmother moved, with her cane wobbling in her hand. *But of course she won't complain. She never does.*

"The new neighbors must have come," said Katie, as she held Gram's chair. "Anyway the shutters are open. Did you see them?"

"Not a thing." Gram sat down slowly, leaning on the table.

"Well, I guess we'll meet them soon enough." If Grandad wouldn't bring it up, Katie would. "And you, Grandad? How did your big, mysterious trip go?" she asked, as soon as he was in his place.

"Pretty well." Grandad's voice was calm, although his smile had faded. "I think I've got things all worked out."

THINGS! Katie could almost see the word, thumping along in capital letters! She eyed him cautiously.

"Katie, your grandmother and I have something to tell you," Grandad continued, strangely solemn, holding the serving fork motionless in his hand. "We've been considering it for some time, and it's definite now." He seemed to be weighing every word. "We don't much like it, and you won't either, but we'll have to face up to it. We're going to move away from Rollins."

All the cozy brightness of the room seemed to fade, as if a lamp had been turned down. "Grandad! You couldn't!" This was worse than anything Katie had thought of. She had heard about being stunned, and she guessed it must feel like this—sort of no feeling at all, with everybody still, while Grandad looked severe, and Gram's hand trembled so hard her cup rattled in its saucer.

After a few shocked moments, Katie's words tumbled out. "I thought it would be practically the end of the world to drown Rollins, but this . . . ! Moving away from my friends! And the ranch! And the rodeos! This is . . . it's *awful*. And what about Whisper?" Her last words were scarcely audible.

"Kathy-girl, I know it's tough, but it can't be helped. I've been thinking about it for some time, and finally found us a place to go. One that's just right."

"Grandad! You can't mean that! No place can be just right, except Rollins."

"We wouldn't go unless we had to. There are reasons, Katie. Think a minute. You know them as well as I do. Your grandmother needs less work."

"Everything will be handy in our new house. We've got it all planned," Katie insisted.

"Even that would be too much for her, nowadays."

"I'll help more, lots more. I'll do all the work, practically."

"I know you'd try," said Grandad gently. "But that's a pretty tall order for someone who has to go to school. I can't do it and run back and forth to the store, too."

Gram thumped her fork on the table. "If my bothersome old bones would only behave! Maybe the new treatments . . ." The hand that held the fork was trembling. "They've shot enough gold into me these past few weeks. Seems as if I ought to be worth something."

"You're not to blame yourself," said Grandad firmly. "We might have to leave in any case." He sighed. "Did you know, Kathy, that Sav-U-Mor is coming?"

"I heard about it, today. I know that's . . . not exactly joyful tidings."

"Hardly. But it's not the only problem. Building a new place—I could hardly manage it at best, even with what the government will pay me." A grim little smile hovered at the corners of his mouth, and Katie could guess what he was thinking—that everyone who had to move was being paid something, but not enough, for the buildings in Rollins were old, and all the settlements were based on value. "I thought over every scheme I could to keep us here, and none of them will work," he continued. "Sav-U-Mor, of course, makes it harder than ever."

The grandfather clock in the hall began to chime, banging and clanging until it seemed to Katie that it would never stop. "*Di-dah*-we-go. *Dun-dah*-so-soon. *Di*-far-a-way."

When it was quiet again, she asked in a small, unsteady voice, "What are we going to do?"

"Move to the city, eventually," said Gram with forced brightness. "Your grandfather heard of a small drug store for sale in the outskirts of Portland, and he went right away to see the owner. He was afraid, if he waited, somebody else might get it."

"And I was in time," said Grandad. "It's just what I've been watching for. Close to a good hospital, for Little Grandmother." This was his tenderest nickname. "Price I can swing. Nice neighborhood. Living quarters in back."

He stopped as if waiting for Katie to say something, but she only stared.

In a moment Grandad sighed and went on talking. "It wasn't actually on the market yet, but another druggist knew what I wanted and telephoned me about it. The owner is retiring next summer, so that will work out just fine. We'll stay here until then. Sell our house and store on the hill—no problem there, with all the new people who want to move in. And when they bulldoze this street—"

"Bulldoze it! This house?" gasped Katie.

It was Grandad's turn to stare. "Of course. Otherwise there'll be chimneys and roofs underwater, to snag boats and fishing lines. What did you expect?"

"I guess—I just didn't think."

"We'll salvage what we can," Grandad explained. "Then they'll 'doze everything flat and burn it."

"But some houses are being moved."

"They're not so old as this one, and they're in better shape."

"If they do that too soon—before you get your new store—what then?" *Maybe it won't work*, Katie was telling herself.

But Grandad only sighed. "Even then we're lucky. Remember the foreman's cabin on your Uncle Steve's ranch? We'll move out there temporarily."

"*Grandad!*" Katie was horrified. "That yucky little shack? Nobody's lived there for ever so long. The windows are all smashed. And—"

"It can be fixed. It has to," Gram said, too cheerfully. "Steve can't house us, with your Aunt Harriet's business sprawled over all their spare rooms. The cabin will do just fine." She passed her cup for more tea. "You've often wished for an adventure, Katie. Well, this will be one, if you'll let it. You can concentrate on the challenge, or you can see nothing but misery. Most adventures depend on a state of mind."

Katie stared at her own hands. That was all very well for Gram to say. She could drink tea anywhere. She wasn't having to leave her school—and the rodeos—and maybe even her horse. "What about Whisper?" she asked.

"Whisper? Well . . . she'll just have to stay at Uncle Steve's, and you can ride her when you come to visit." Grandad was speaking heavily, and the lines on his face were deep. "Kathy-girl, I know it isn't ideal, but it's the best we can manage."

"Then—when—?"

"Soon as we can, we'll move to Portland," Grandad answered, his voice still sad. "With a part-time clerk, and the apartment right there in back, I can give Little Grandmother the help she needs. We'll be snug as three bugs in a rug and you'll soon learn to like your new school."

"This may not be what any of us would choose," added Gram rather tartly. "But it's the best plan we've been able to figure out, and we've done quite a lot of figuring."

Grandad adopted a bantering tone. "You know I'm quite a chef! I've always said a short-order joint would be my second choice, next to a pharmacy. So I'll be the family cook."

At this Katie jumped up and let her napkin slide to the floor. "It's *awful*!" she wailed. "*Awful*! I know you're trying to make it sound like a lark to help me, but it doesn't help. It doesn't. Nothing could make it right to leave Rollins. And I can't keep Whisper in training—or ride in any more rodeos—or anything. It isn't fair!"

With a clatter and bang she gathered up her dishes and took them to the sink.

4

The Girl with the Yellow Kitten

I won't cry—I won't, thought Katie as she scraped and stacked the dishes. *Why did I burst out like that? Why can't I, just once, keep my feelings to myself?*

"I'm sorry—really and truly I am—for yelling," she said. "I guess we'll . . . we'll . . . get along . . . all right." Her voice sounded so shaky that she turned on lots of hot water to drown it out.

Just as she washed the last cooking dish, the doorbell pinged, and Mrs. Wylam, from two houses away, came to spend the evening with Gram. Somehow Katie managed to chat with her for a moment, then walked back to the store with her grandfather, for all the restaurants and ice cream parlors needed extra help tonight. They passed the Sanders Hardware, the barber shop, the Golden Quail Cafe, and the Rollins Hotel, with its battered, swinging sign. Here many of the cowboys would sleep, three to a bed or rolled up in sleeping bags on the floor.

In the drugstore people were already sitting on the wire-backed chairs and standing three-deep at the counters.

"This won't last long, just till the dance begins," said Brad, as he rinsed a scoop and made a butter brickle ice cream cone. "But there's plenty to do right now. Two banana splits, for starters."

Katie began to peel the bananas.

Cowboys—fragrant with shaving lotion, for they were ready for the Cowboy Dance—were crowding all the tables. "Something special, Katie, for a starving cowpoke?" one of them asked. "Chocolate chip?"

Another began to laugh. "Chocolate Chip! I drew a bronc named that today, and he just about chipped me! But good!"

Katie tried to enter as she always did into their banter, but tonight she could hardly find the words. *We're moving! We're moving! We have to leave Rollins!* It was a horrid chant, tumbling along over and over in her thoughts. How could Grandad be so calm, and Gram talk so glibly about adventures and states of mind? One thing was sure. She wouldn't do it. No matter what. She couldn't even bear to think about it, and *someway, somehow,* she was going to figure out *something.* It was a good thing Gram couldn't peer into the state of her mind right then.

At the first chance she followed Brad to the private room behind the pharmacy counter. "You knew, didn't you?" she said softly, so nobody could hear.

"Well, Grandad told me what was on his mind, but he hadn't decided for sure and didn't want to get you upset for nothing."

"Upset!" blazed Katie. "For *nothing!* You'll be in college—maybe it's nothing to you. But I'll have to leave all my friends, my school—everything."

Tight-lipped, Brad interrupted. "*Your* school. *Your* friends. What about Grandad's store, and his friends that he's had his whole life? And his garden? And Gram—maybe drinking tea isn't very important to you, but it is to her. She can't get around much to meet new people."

"But—but . . ." stammered Katie.

"Of course it's tough for you," Brad continued, more mildly. "But Grandad doesn't want to go, either. Do you think he's happy about it?"

"I know he isn't." Katie's tears were almost spilling over. "But Brad . . . he's just given up. If he'd only make up his mind to stay, no matter what—If he'd really tried."

"He's tried." Brad's face was serious as he picked up a prescription that Grandad had prepared. "He's scared of Sav-U-More. Business is pretty good right now, with construction workers all over the place, but as soon as the dam is done, they'll move on."

"Grandad is friends with everybody from the town and ranches, too. They'd stick by him," insisted Katie. "Maybe he'll change his mind." Although she squared her shoulders and put on a smile as she followed Brad into the hubbub of the front room, her stomach felt hollow, and she couldn't forget Brad's words. *He was right*, she thought. *Grandad's leaving a lot, too, and Gram would be lonesome, anyplace but here. I was mean. I didn't think about them at all.*

Late that evening, leaving Brad to take care of the after-the-dance crowd, Katie and Grandad went home together, both lost in thought, finding little to say. When they reached the house, they found Gram still up.

"Gram, I shouldn't have burst out like that," Katie exclaimed, dropping onto the sofa close to her rocking chair. "I know moving is hard for you, too. I just didn't think."

"We all look at life through a mirror," Gram replied in her tart, brisk voice. "And the main thing we see is our own reflection."

"Yes . . . well . . . I really am sorry about your friends, too. And Grandad—your garden. You were going to move your plants to our new house."

"I still can keep some of them, the best ones.

There's a bit of ground behind the store, and another along the sidewalk," Grandad replied.

"And there's no use fussing." Gram was rocking again. "We have to do it—so we will." She began asking about the evening. Yes, Katie told her, they'd been busy. Yes, a lot of her friends had come in. They were all praising Whisper.

"I'm pretty tired," she finished, with a sigh.

"It's been a busy day," Gram agreed.

"Right. Goodnight, now," Katie said, and ran upstairs with Tully at her heels.

When she first came to live there, she had chosen the tower room for her own. Most of it was in the main house, but the tower jutted out to form a circular bay of high, narrow windows in pairs, each with a deep window seat below. This was her retreat, a place to curl up with a good book, a place to weep when things were going wrong, a place to storm out her troubles, a place to dream.

Sadly she now slipped into pajamas and corduroy robe and sprawled on the high walnut bed, while Tully watched from his basket in the corner. She gazed at the rose-patterned paper, the small-paned windows, the funny little jog where the roof line came down almost to the floor. Smashed . . . burned . . . *Everything will be gone*, she thought. But even tonight, when Tully hopped to the floor and brought her his tattered old sock tied in knots, she held it by one end while he gripped the other and shook it ferociously, flapping his ears and growling through his teeth.

"Silly!" Katie said with a shaky laugh. "Do you think it's a rat?"

At last, feeling tired but somehow not ready for sleep, she turned out the light and curled up in the window seat. Inside, moonlight laid a silver rectangle on the floor. Outside, she could see the big side yard with its hedge, rose bed and plaster statue of St. Francis, white under the moon.

A Kathleen day, she thought. She liked her name, which could be anything she chose. Hardly anyone said it in full, Katherine, but whenever she thought of it that way she felt marvelously grownup and dignified. Then there was Katie for everyday. Kate when she "fell apart." Brad often called her that. Kathy, Grandad's favorite, which made her feel cherished. Kay, crisp and capable. And Kathleen, like the song:

Oh, I will take you back, Kathleen,
To where your heart will feel no pain.

She wondered whether the Kathleen in the song could possibly feel as much pain as she did right now, at the thought of leaving her darling Whisper Please.

She'd had her such a long time. She could remember everything right back to when Whisper was a newborn foal. "You can't train her yet," Uncle Steve had said. "She's too young. Let her grow up first."

But Katie hadn't been able to wait. Not that she'd argued—she knew better than to argue with Uncle Steve. Instead, she'd done everything she could to win the trust of Whisper's mother. She'd moved slowly and spoken softly, petted her a lot, brought her carrots and apples. Pretty soon she could lead Whisper around by the mane, sometimes laying an old gunny sack across her back, like a saddle. When Whisper was used to that, she'd found a little pony halter to try and Whisper didn't mind.

So one Sunday she said, "I've got a surprise for you, Uncle Steve. Will you come down to the corral with me?"

"Well . . . sure," Uncle Steve replied, with his usual grin. And he really had been surprised when she led out her very own foal, to follow along like a little dog, picking up her hooves so neatly and bobbing her head.

But now, Katie thought, *she couldn't—she couldn't possibly leave her precious horse, just when she was finally old enough to ride. How could she go to live in a horrid city and hardly ever see Whisper at all?* Just thinking about it made her flop down on the bed and bury her face in the pillow.

She sat up straight, however, when she heard a faint wail from somewhere outside. Startled, she ran to the window, cupped her hands around her eyes and peered into the dark. In a moment it came again: a plaintive "mew," at which Tully jumped onto the windowseat and woofed.

"S-sh! It's only a kitten!" Katie told him, still trying to see out. "It's probably climbed a tree and can't get down."

At another mew Tully barked again.

"Hush!" commanded Katie. "I'm going after it. Now you keep quiet, or you'll wake everybody up." Putting on shoes, she crept down the stairs, carefully stepping over the squeaky tread.

In the next yard, lighted by moonlight, she soon discovered two luminous green eyes staring at her from high up in a cottonwood tree. A kitten for sure, she thought, and wanted to rescue it, but she found the lowest branch just out of reach. While she was trying to figure out what to do, a round spot of light appeared and grew steadily larger. A trespasser? Burglar? One of the new neighbors? Cautiously Katie slipped behind the tree and waited until the intruder moved into a patch of moonlight. It was a girl about her own age, in pajamas and coat, walking slowly and shining her flashlight all around.

"This is the one it's in," said Katie, emerging from behind the tree.

"Oh!" The girl nearly dropped the light.

"It's all right. I heard the kitten and came to investigate. And when I saw your light, I hid."

"Oh!" said the girl again. Then she giggled. "So we both scared each other!" At another plaintive "mew," she looked upward. "Poor little Chrys. He's always getting himself treed. Since I've had him I'm turning into a regular fireman. Only this time we don't have a ladder." She had a high, light voice with a breathy catch in it, as if she were about to laugh.

"We have one," said Katie. "I'll get it, while you keep watch, in case he climbs down."

Soon she was back with a ladder bumping along behind her. "No matter what system I try, I sound like a gravel truck. I hope I haven't wakened my family," she said, as she tried to prop the ladder against the tree.

"It looks heavy," said the girl, still with that catch of laughter.

"It is. But maybe we can raise it together, if we set one end about here . . ."

"And both of us push."

Panting, they finally had it in place. "Twice when I tried this, I fell off," said the girl, with one foot on the bottom rung. "I suppose that makes me utterly unfit to own a kitten like Chrys. Do you mind steadying it—the ladder, I mean?"

"Not a bit," Katie replied. "Do you think he'll scratch? If he's so scared?"

"I don't think so. He's used to being plucked out of trees. He's a candidate for Most Rescued Cat." Laughing, the girl began to climb.

In a moment she came down with the kitten clawing at her shoulder. "Chrys? Is that his name?" asked Katie, stroking his head.

"His name is Chrysanthemum. Because he's yellow, and when he's excited, such as now, his fur sticks out like petals."

"It does at that. He's a darling. He must be pretty young."

"Three months." The girl began to tickle his chin. "Do you have a cat?"

"Just a dog that thinks he's people." Katie told her about Tully and his sock.

The girl sighed. "You're lucky. I love Chrys, of course—but I'd love a dog, too. Only my mom wouldn't. The only reason I have Chrys is because he's little and quiet and generally out of sight." She began to laugh again. "Even getting him was a major victory." As if he understood, Chrys began to purr.

"Are you from the new family next door?" Katie asked.

"That's right. We rented the house sight unseen, furniture and all, just until we find one to buy. I've never lived in anything like it—all dark hallways and jigs and jogs."

"It's the oldest one in town, next to ours," said Katie.

"Is it—maybe—haunted?" The girl sounded hopeful.

"Not haunted. Just old."

Although they shivered in the chilly night air, they lingered for a few minutes, talking. Katie learned that the girl's name was Allison Trudeau and that she was also in the eighth grade. Even in the moonlight Katie could see that she was about her own height. *So I won't be the only short one*, she thought. *That will be fun.*

An only child, Allison had lived in foreign countries all her life, moving from one to another, wherever her father's job as engineer took them. "I've had lots of Japanese friends, Austrian, Malaysian," said Allison, with the laughter gone from her voice. "And of course other American kids like me, who move around with their dads. But this will be my first time in a real American school. I'm kind of scared, but still I hope we can stay here forever. I'm *utterly* tired of walking into new schools and being stared at. It's awful, being a stranger all the time."

I was one once, thought Katie, remembering the year she came to Rollins. She'd been in the second grade then, and she'd never forget how it felt to have not even one friend, with so many strange faces and names to keep straight, and everybody talking among themselves about things she'd never heard of.

Taking Chrys, she cuddled him in the crook of her arm. "I suppose you know about our big flood," she said.

"My dad told me. It's creepy."

"That's what a lot of people think. Some are leaving. My best friend Judy, who lived in your house, has moved away for good."

"It's so sad—utterly heartbreaking—to lose a friend," murmured Allison. "And you—are you moving too?"

Katie hesitated. "We . . . ? Well, of course. Everyone is." Pulling the kitten off her shoulder, she handed it over. "There's a rodeo this weekend. Want to go with me tomorrow?"

Allison caught her breath. "To the rodeo? We saw the signs—and some cowboys." She giggled. "They're cute! We ate dinner at the hotel dining room tonight, and cowboys were all over the place. They look so funny, eating with those big hats on, sort of perched on the backs of their heads."

"Cowboys always eat that way. They like to. Besides . . ." Katie began to laugh, her first really good laugh since Grandad had told her his plan. "Can you imagine fifty of those big hats, all hung up on pegs, and so much alike?"

"Complete chaos!" agreed Allison. "Is this a real rodeo? Like I've read about?"

"It's real, all right. I rode in the barrel race today."

"You rode? How *utterly* exciting! Do you own your horse? What's its name?"

"Yes—and yes." Katie was laughing again. "I rode my own horse. Her name is Whisper Please, because she has such a whiffly little nicker. And she's a nibbler. Carrots, my fingers, my hair. She doesn't bite, just chews with her lips, and they tickle."

"How perfect!" Allison murmured. "Are you riding tomorrow?"

"Just watching. I'll stop by for you, if you'd like to go."

"Oh, I can't imagine anything more utterly thrilling."

"Okay." Katie stroked Chrys one last time. "But I'm just about frozen. 'Night, then."

" 'Night." The kitten mewed again as Allison scurried across the yard toward her own house.

I won't miss Judy quite so much with Allison here, thought Katie.

As she passed through the garden, moonlight still shone on the statue of St. Francis and cast deep shadows between the plaster folds of his gown. I should have explained that we're moving entirely away, not just to the new town, she thought. But I couldn't say it. Not yet, when the idea is all so new. After all, we'll be here for a long time. I'll tell her about it, the first good chance.

And we left the ladder. Oh, well, Allison will help me carry it back tomorrow. It will be fun to do it together.

Teeth chattering from the cold, she ran into the house, climbed into bed, and pulled the covers up around her ears.

5

Lookout Rock

The next day Allison's father, a big, smiling, quiet man, took them to the rodeo early and let them go in by themselves. Allison was entranced by everything, especially the barrel race, which was ridden today by young women past their teens.

"You did that!" she kept exclaiming to Katie. "I'm utterly impressed! Do you think I could learn it? Maybe ride next year?"

"Of course you can, if you get a horse," Katie replied. *And I'll be riding too*, she told herself. *I'll find a way*.

Seen by daylight, Allison was a little taller than Katie and not quite so slender, with short, curly dark hair and fair skin. She kept a bottle of lotion in her jeans bag and smeared it on whenever they went outside. "Otherwise I'd be a regular beet," she explained. "Burn and peel, burn and peel. That's me."

They stayed until the last horse was ridden, then walked home together. "I can see I'm going to have really strong legs, living here," said Allison with a giggle.

"We walk a lot," Katie agreed.

On Monday Allison eagerly enrolled in the eighth grade. "I knew an American school would be different, and I really wanted to go to one, but I was kind of scared," she confessed while they were having lunch in the noisy cafeteria. "And now . . . it's even better than I hoped." She had signed up for soccer, and Linda had steered her to the chorus, which was already beginning practice for a gigantic pageant.

"I get chills all up and down my backbone every time I think of it," she continued, pouring out a pool of ketchup. "It sounds utterly tremendous. Linda says she's going to be in the square dances and that you're riding Whisper."

"Away out on the hills, with a lot of other riders, and even some covered wagons, all lighted by search-lights—sort of a farewell to the old town. I found a sidesaddle in Uncle Steve's barn, so I'm trying to get used to it." Katie laughed and rubbed her knee. "It may look romantic, but it's really just plain misery."

"Doesn't Linda ride?"

"She *can*, but she'd rather sing or be in a play."

"Oh. Well, I'm going to sing with her. And tomorrow I'll have my first swimming class." Allison began to gather up her dishes. "Do you like to swim?"

"No." Katie replied, so bluntly that Allison gave her an inquiring look. But Katie never talked about her parents, and now she only added, as casually as she could, "I never go in unless our P.E. class has to." The mention of swimming had brought back that long-ago accident in the boat, and the sudden storm. Sometimes, even yet, she had nightmares of monster waves and the shock of cold water, of drifting on and on in a gray world, all alone. She'd been seven at the time, the only one who wore a life jacket, the only one saved.

Now, seeing Allison's troubled expression, she hastily changed the subject. "Want to see our Lookout Rock? I'll ask some others, and we'll have an expedition."

"Wonderful!"

However, the expedition shrank, because most of their classmates had to leave on the bus, or had a doctor's appointment, or a baby-sitting job.

Linda, however, was unexpectedly free. "I can go with you, if you won't be too long," she said. "My ballet class is canceled, and my dad isn't planning to pick me up until late."

"That's great," Katie said, giving her arm a squeeze.

When their classes were over, the three set out and soon were clambering up a faint path that angled back and forth on one of the treeless hills. They climbed—rested—climbed again. Grasping a clump of antelope brush, Allison pulled herself to a flat spot by the trail, where she took off her jacket and tied it around her waist by its sleeves. "I'll bet I'm purple!" she exclaimed, bringing out her lotion.

"Just about! I expect I am, too," said Katie.

"But if you think it's hot now, you should try it in summer," added Linda, her braces glittering in the sun. "It's enough to melt you right down to a blob."

"It looks awfully high," said Allison doubtfully, as she gazed at the gray outcropping above them.

"Oh, we won't climb all the way to the rim-rock. I never got that far unless I'm on Whisper. The lookout is just ahead." Katie pointed to a large flat boulder surrounded by twisted, gray-green sage. "We'll be there before you know it."

"Good! I hardly have one single molecule of oxygen left in me! I'm utterly out of breath."

When they reached the boulder, they scrambled up, lay flat on their stomachs, and peered over the edge. The rock was warm, the air sharp with the tang of sagebrush, and the breeze lifted their hair. They could see all up and down the Columbia River, silvery gray, flecked by whitecaps, and bordered on both sides by bare, brown, rolling hills. Far below was the jagged slit of Bone Creek, with Rollins spread along both banks. The girls spotted the slanting roof of Allison's house, the bay windows and tower of Katie's, the school, churches, stores, and higher up, the raw-lumber yellow of houses that were being built on the hills.

"The new town is in rattlesnake country now, but the snakes will leave when the people move in—or at least we hope they will," Katie explained, which made Allison shudder.

"Down there, on those tracks away out over the river," Linda said, "that's the shoo-fly railroad. They have to move it to high ground, and with so much blasting, they put the rails out there for a while, safe from falling rocks."

"What a job!" murmured Allison. She pointed to a deep, shadowed gash that ran back from the river, into the hills. "What's that?"

"Stone Canyon," Katie explained. "That's Stone River in it. And there, on the far side of the canyon up in that high draw, that's Uncle Steve's ranch, where I keep Whisper. See—there's the barn . . . corral . . . house. And that little building, the brown one, just this side of the main house, is part of the Double Bar S, too. When it was a working ranch, that was the foreman's cabin." *That's where I'm supposed to move*, she thought. *Right there to that stupid little yucky house. And then to an even yuckier city.*

"Is it a real ranch? A big one?" asked Allison.

"It was big, once. My Aunt Harriet's great-great-grandfather—well, I'm not sure how many 'greats' it was, but he settled there when he came west. After he died, his relatives sold most of the land, so Uncle Steve and Aunt Harriet got part of it, to raise some horses.

"A ranch—a real ranch," murmured Allison. "You're lucky, Katie. But is it going to be flooded, too?"

"Only the low section, not the buildings. See those strips of bare dirt below the house? That's where the new road and railroad are coming. Aunt Harriet hates them. She says they'll ruin what little peace and quiet she has left."

"I want to see it close up, especially that little cabin. It looks neat, like a mystery!" exclaimed Allison in her breathy voice.

"It isn't, really. Just old and crummy." *And it's dismal! And it's mine!* Katie added to herself. How could her friends not hear the thoughts that were banging around inside her head! How could they be so practically breathless with excitement, not disgusted at all. "And there's the Terrible Dam," she added. "Away off, past the place where the river narrows."

Allison squinted into the light. "It looks so small!"

"Grandad says it's already more than a hundred feet high."

"Big enough to drown our whole town," added Linda.

"And turn everything crossways."

"Crossways?" said Allison. "When everything will be nice and new, and you're all moving together?"

"The same *people* will be there," Katie replied. "But the old school and the rodeo ring and Bone Creek, and the trees—they'll all be gone. Besides, everybody's having a great big feud. The grownups, that is, not the kids."

"They squabble over who gets which lot," Linda explained.

"Make committees. Go campaigning," Katie added. "Get people to sign petitions. Aunt Harriet has been to Washington twice, and Uncle Steve says her telephone bills will bankrupt him for sure."

Using her jacket for a pillow, Katie gazed at the sky where a hawk soared in lazy circles, then screamed and dived into the river valley. Bare, rounded, the hills on the other side of the Columbia rolled in swirls and drifts of color: black bluffs, gray-green sage, autumn brown range grass, with cattle as small as dots on the high range.

BOOM! The explosion was louder than thunder, a sudden tremendous blast that echoed from the hills.

Allison sat bolt upright. "Oh! What happened?"

"Just the Daily Bang," said Katie, wrinkling her nose. "It happens once every morning and once every afternoon. I don't know how they missed the first one today."

"Unless it was the rodeo," Linda suggested. "The workers might be tired out and haven't accomplished as much as usual.

"But—but what *was* it?" Allison's voice trembled.

"They drill lots of holes and put explosives into the rocks down there, to blast for the road. Then they set it all off at once. It shakes the whole town: rattles dishes, knocks bricks out of chimneys, cracks windows."

"Such a lot of dust!" Allison grimaced at the yellow cloud. "It's practically a mushroom!"

"And it never really settles. We've had grit on everything for years," Katie told her. "When we're having company, even if we dust the last minute before they come, you can still write your name on the tables. Gram says it seems as if the dustcloth will grow to her hand."

Allison's voice was still shaky. "I was just about utterly scared out of my wits."

"You'll never get used to it," said Katie. "None of us has." *I've got to tell them*, she thought, *or it isn't being quite honest*. She looked away and forced herself to continue. "Allison . . . Linda . . . that little house on Uncle Steve's ranch—the crummy one . . . Grandad is planning to move there." Her next words came out in a mumble. "And then to Portland."

Linda sat upright. "Portland! But, Katie! You can't go! Just when we're ready for high school! Just when we're going to the same classes and try out together for the plays. It won't be half as much fun without you!" Her round face was wide-eyed with dismay.

Allison also stared. "I thought your grandfather was building on the hills, same as everyone else."

"He is. But he's going to sell out. He doesn't think he can keep a store going here and take care of Gram." Try as she would, Katie couldn't quite keep the quiver out of her voice as she told Allison about Gram's arthritis and the coming of Sav-U-Mor.

"Can't you do anything about it?" Allison exclaimed. "Help your grandmother? Earn some money? You can't just sit still—and—and wait for it to happen."

"I've already offered. But no luck." Katie didn't even try to describe the dreadful hollow in her stomach.

"There's got to be something," insisted Allison.

"I've thought about it ever since Grandad told me. You couldn't imagine the schemes I've dreamed up. Starting a baby-sitting service. Washing cars. A doggie boutique." Katie tried to make it sound like a joke. "So far I haven't found anything that's even halfway sensible. But I'm not giving up."

She glanced at the sky. "Look, Linda. The sun's going down, and we'd better start back, so you can meet your dad. I have to help Gram get dinner, too. She's the best cook ever at all the sitting-down jobs, but she can't walk very much, so I fetch and carry." She started down the path, with the others close behind. "Allison," she called over her shoulder as she picked her way along. "You can really see a lot more from the rimrock. Want to ride up there?"

"I'd love it, only I don't have a horse."

"Uncle Steve has plenty. He'll lend you—oh—Sugar Plum. Or Lacey Lady. She's Whisper's mother. Can you ride, Allison?"

"I've ridden in riding schools in Austria, but never on a mountain." Laughter had returned to Allison's voice. "It sounds great."

"Then I'll ask Brad for one. Will your mother mind?" Katie stopped in the speckled shade of a mesquite bush to catch her breath.

"If I explain it right, I'm sure she'll say yes," Allison declared. "She'll give me stacks of advice and make me wear enough clothes to keep three people warm, but she'll let me go. When shall we? Some weekend pretty soon?"

"Not *some* weekend. *This* weekend. Saturday. Can you make it then, Linda? I'll borrow a horse for you, too, so you needn't bother to bring Nutmeg."

"No way," Linda replied, with a mournful shake of her head. "I've always got to go to the dentist on Saturday. Every week, practically forever."

"Well . . . I really wish you could. But Allison, shall you and I go anyway? Take a picnic and spend the day?"

"Perfect!" Allison broke off a sprig of mesquite

and turned it thoughtfully in her hand. "At least, it would be perfect, if you didn't have to move."

"I'm not gone yet," said Katie, as they started on down the path. "Gram always says while there's life there's hope."

But "hope" isn't the right word, she told herself as she moved cautiously along. *What I need is more like grim determination. That, and maybe some good luck, too.*

6

Stone Canyon

Katie was up early on Saturday, so she could scurry through the house-cleaning and have a long day on Whisper. "We're going away up to the rimrock," she told Gram. "I think Allison will love it."

"Can she ride?" asked Gram, as she limped around with her perennial dustcloth.

"Well . . . some, anyway. I asked Brad, and he said she could take steady old Sugar Plum."

However, while Katie was in the kitchen packing a lunch, the telephone rang, and Allison's breathless voice came over the wire. "I'm devastated. Utterly wiped out. But I can't go after all. My parents have to shop for the house—curtains and things like that—so they're driving to Portland for the weekend. And they're taking me along."

"You could stay overnight with me," Katie suggested. "That is, if you'd like to."

"Oh, I'd *like* to," Allison sadly replied. "But this is my only chance to buy school clothes, and my Malaysian things aren't right for here, and if I leave it to my Mom—well, I want to pick them out myself. But maybe . . . do you think we could ride next weekend instead?"

"Easily. This time of year the weather is almost always okay."

"Then that's all right," said Allison with a sigh of relief.

Katie turned away from the telephone. "What a letdown," she said. "I thought it was all set."

Gram had just begun a crossword puzzle. "Ancient time-keeper. In two words," she murmured. "S-U—sun dial, of course." After penciling in the letters, she glanced up at Katie. "It's disappointing, but you can go anyway," she said. "Land knows, there's plenty of horsey girls to keep you company. And Bonnie Wylam is coming over for a cup of tea, so I won't be alone."

However, some of Katie's friends weren't home, and the rest were busy, so in the end she decided to go by herself. Feeling rather forlorn, she tied her hair back for coolness, picked up her hat and boots, and started on foot to the ranch.

She wasn't surprised to find it deserted, for on

Saturday morning Uncle Steve was always at his office, and Brad helped Grandad in the store. As for Aunt Harriet . . . she was heels-over-head in the New Rollins Steering Committee, with its endless meetings. No matter. Katie was used to handling Whisper, so she brushed and saddled her quickly and sprayed her legs for flies. Just as she started to put on her too-tight boots, she noticed an outgrown pair of Brad's lying under a bench. They're big enough, that's sure—regular duck's feet, she thought with a giggle, slipping them on. But they were so much more comfortable than her own that she decided to wear them anyway.

As Whisper jogged merrily along, Katie's melancholy vanished, for the day was bright, with a warm, sagebrush-scented breeze. Just before the lane started its long downward slope, she rode out onto a ridge that overlooked the Columbia. There she stopped, to wait quietly in the sun.

No house was in sight, no barn, no corral, no person—just the river and the brown hills, and herself on Whisper, feeling as if the world belonged to her, and she could do anything she chose. This must be how it seemed to be grown up. Big. Strong. In charge.

She glanced back at the rimrock, high above her, hot under the sun and lacking even a speck of shade. Stone Canyon would be cool, she thought, lots more comfortable than the burned-dry hills, and it had looked so mysterious and dark, seen from the lookout.

She could go there now. Yes, that's what she would do.

When she came to the main road, instead of heading for the hills, she turned right and soon entered the shadowy gorge, with its jagged walls of dark gray basalt. Almost at once the sounds of traffic faded, and she could hear only the splash of Stone River and twittering of birds. It was cool, as she had hoped, with a stronger breeze here, blowing across the stream. Willows cast a lacy shade. Gray water ouzels, their nesting season over, were bobbing in the shallows, and bank swallows were darting back and forth.

Katie let Whisper pick her way upstream. At a curve where the rock walls close together, she looked up and up, to two bridges under construction—a rough railroad trestle, and a graceful concrete span for the highway. It was white, pure, seeming to soar like a butterfly. Could the water possibly rise so high? Uncle Steve's ranch was up there, close to the bridges, but back from the edge and out of sight.

Just past the bridges, Katie came to a small feeder-stream that foamed around the base of an enormous black boulder. Here she cautiously guided Whisper into her favorite side canyon, a small one that soon widened into a rocky circle, like a room. Here a ribbon of water curled over a high ledge and thundered into a dark pool. A wren fluttered up as she passed; a tan-and-black ground squirrel scampered across the rocks.

"Thirsty?" Katie asked, halting beside the pool. Whisper plunged her muzzle into the water, making dribbly sounds, while a cold, wet wind blew from the falls and lifted Katie's hair.

BOOM! The ground shook and stones rattled down the slopes.

"We can't escape it, even here," Katie remarked to Whisper, who snuffled and waggled an ear.

"Lunchtime," she continued, "and I'm starved." A few steps away from the pool she dismounted and let the reins fall forward to the ground. Whisper at once began to graze, but just as Katie reached for her sandwiches and fruit, she noticed a clump of speckled yellow blossoms growing head-high on the rocky bank. They were monkey flowers, paler than usual and later-blooming, and she wanted to see them close up.

Impulsively she began to climb, teetering on the treacherous stones. While she was reaching for a handhold and half out of balance, something rattled. A snake! she thought. It sounded almost underfoot. Jerking back and looking wildly around, she spotted it at once, not more than a yard away and coiled, with its forked tongue darting in and out. Frantically she stepped sideways—onto a loose stone. It rolled. Pebbles clattered. Trying to keep from falling, she swung her arms in panic, just as her foot, in its oversized boot, slipped off the rock.

She heard a thud, a snap, and tumbled headlong, while fingers of fire seemed to seize her ankle. All in a blur she saw the snake slithering away, and Whisper peacefully continuing to graze.

Except for the roar of the waterfall, everything was quiet, as Katie lay flat on the rocks, unable to move. She seemed to be floating in a fog . . . rising . . . falling . . . spinning. Gritting her teeth, she tried to sit up, and finally, by shutting her eyes and dragging herself sideways, she managed to prop herself against a knobby boulder.

My boot—I've got to take it off—I know that much, she thought, although even the gentlest tug pierced her like the thrust of a dagger. *I've got to . . . before it swells,* she told herself again, bending forward and grasping her ankle. *It's a good thing I wore Brad's boots instead of my own tight ones.* But no matter how gingerly she moved, the stab of sudden pain made her so dizzy that she braced both hands against the ground and shut her eyes.

As soon as things were clear again, she wedged the boot heel between two rocks and pulled—and nearly blacked out—and pulled again. *I can't,* she thought, as tears rolled down her face. *It hurts too much.* But, biting her tongue, she slid her foot a scant quarter-inch—and another—and at last she scooped it past the tight throat of the boot.

As if through a fog, she stared at her ankle, which

was bent quite out of shape. *Broken. It must be*, she vaguely thought, as slowly, trying not to jar her leg, she lay down on the warm, pebbly canyon floor. She'd think what to do—at least she'd try to—but later on. She had to rest first.

After some time—she had no idea how long—she roused enough to realize what had happened. Cooling it . . . that was supposed to be the best thing to do for a break. She tried to move, gasped, and clutched the nearest rock. However, the stream was so close that, by sliding along—with many stops—she managed to reach its edge and lower her foot into the water.

Although at first it seemed like touching a cake of ice, Katie slowly felt a blessed numbness creep over her injured leg, and as the throbbing eased, her brain began to clear. The important thing, she realized, the thing she simply had to figure out, was how to get away from the canyon. Surely that wouldn't be very difficult, with Whisper so near to carry her home. Confidently she turned herself halfway around and called, "Whisper—good girl—here. Come here now."

The horse raised her head and looked up, ears pricked.

"Here, girl. Come along." Seeing a bunch of blue delphinium within arm's reach, Katie pulled them up and waved them enticingly. "Good Whisper . . . please . . . *please*, Whisper . . . come here."

The horse moved toward her and nibbled at the

flowers, while Katie drew them slowly closer until she could grasp a stirrup. Holding it with both hands, she raised herself a few inches—a few more—until she could get her uninjured leg under her, and at last, with a mighty tug on the stirrup, she stood up, clutching the saddle horn and swaying.

But when she tried to mount, she found that she could neither stand on the broken foot, nor place it in the stirrup and use it to swing herself up. She balanced herself on her sound leg, held the saddle with both hands, pulled with all her strength—and failed.

I can usually do push-ups, she told herself. At least a few. Tears were streaming down her face. Maybe . . . if it didn't hurt so much. For a moment she laid her cheek against the warm saddle, smelling of leather. Then she tried again, and at last sank down on the ground, still clinging to the stirrup.

Once more, she seemed to be floating in a fog. She was alone, and she couldn't ride Whisper after all. But it was up to her—nobody else—to figure a way out. So . . . what to do?

She could raise the reins and send Whisper away, in hopes she'd go home. But even if Brad or Uncle Steve found the riderless horse, they would think she had been riding on her favorite rimrock trail and look for her there.

Did Gram know where she was? Not a chance, for she had changed her plans at the last minute.

Maybe she could tie on a note. However, a search

of her pockets turned up nothing to write with. She was caught. Unless, somehow, she let them know where she was, they would be so sure she'd headed for the hills that it might take hours—it might take days—for them to find her.

Should she send up a smoke column? Even if she could gather wood, she had no way to light a fire. Float something down the stream? What could possibly have any meaning? She had only Whisper to take a message.

Looking vaguely around, she noticed a nearby clump of willows, growing beside the stream. Willows . . . WILLOWS! Suddenly she knew what to do, and it was so simple. Why, she wondered, didn't she think of it sooner?

"Do you know that sometimes you have a very dumb mistress?" she asked, holding tightly to the stirrup.

Gasping with pain, Katie then pulled herself to her feet, grabbed the saddle with both hands, and had Whisper help her to the willow, where she tore off a bunch of shoots. It's lucky I tied back my hair, she thought, as she used the ribbon to fasten them to the saddlehorn. Stream beds were the only places where willows grew, and this canyon was the nearest one that was wide enough for riding. She would send Whisper home, and whoever found her would know she'd come from a canyon, not the rimrock.

"Whisper, my darling Whisper, it's all up to you," she said.

Pulling up the reins, she twisted them firmly around the saddle horn, so they couldn't fall forward and trip the horse. Then, after one last tug to make sure the willow was secure, she put all the weight on her sound leg, released the reins and, almost fainting with pain, gave Whisper a sharp slap on the rump.

"Now go!" she shouted. "Go home! Find Brad! Find Uncle Steve! Find somebody!" Waving her arms, she yelled at the top of her voice until she fell down all in a heap, while the mare snorted and flung up her head. She waited for a moment, trotted a few feet, stopped and looked back.

"Go on—go—go—run!" Katie shouted.

Whisper moved along the gravel, pausing often to chomp down a tender bunch of grass.

"Run!" Katie threw a rock. But she was lying on the ground, and the rock fell short. Whisper only flicked an ear, then moved with maddening slowness from one bunch of green to another, until at last she rounded the black rock toward the main canyon. Toward home, Katie hoped. Toward freedom for her.

With Whisper gone, the canyon was lonely. A ground squirrel chirred. The waterfall roared. High in the blue sky a circling hawk screamed and dived.

Katie eased herself to the stream and once more plunged her aching foot into the cold water. Would Whisper go all the way home? she wondered. Were the willow branches tied well enough? Would anybody figure out what they meant? The sun was hot, her foot was screaming at her, and she was tired. So tired. Leaning back against the lumpy boulder, she closed her eyes.

A long time afterward, when the sun had crossed the top of the sky and was shining from the opposite rim of the canyon, she heard the clatter of hooves and a shout. "Katie! Katie! Are you there?"

"Here! Around the black rock!" she yelled. "Help me!"

"Coming!" called the voice—Brad's voice—and at the familiar sound Katie felt as if she were dissolving inside.

Soon he came in sight, riding Britches and leading Whisper. "Katie! You're hurt!" he exclaimed at sight of her foot dangling in the pool.

"Broken, I think," she replied, trying to keep calm. "And—oh, Brad—it feels awful. And I was afraid you wouldn't find me . . . and I tied on the willow . . . and Whisper didn't want to go . . . and. . . ." *I won't cry. I won't*, she fiercely told herself, clenching her hands. *I've managed this far.*

"Now take it easy. I'll get you home." Brusque as Brad's words were, his voice was gentle. "A splint, I think. That will ease the pain. Good thing I was a

Boy Scout." He began to search the ground, up and down the banks of the stream.

While he hunted, he told her that a neighbor, Matt Hewitt, had found Whisper nibbling bunch grass along the road, almost at the entrance to their lane. "A riderless horse means trouble," Brad said, "and Hewitt recognized Whisper, so he telephoned me at the store. It was easy enough to figure out what the willow meant—smart move, Kate—and here I am."

In a few minutes he brought two strips of wood. "These'll work," he said. "Can you turn so I can tie them on?"

"I—I think so." Katie slid away from the pool. As gently as possible, Brad straightened the injured foot, laid the wood against it, and wrapped it with his handkerchief, while Katie bit her tongue, determined not to cry out.

"Better?" he asked, when he was finished.

"Lots better. That splint really helps." Katie felt steadier now that the pain was somewhat relieved.

"How'd you get into this fix, anyway?" asked Brad as he tied the final knot.

"I wasn't careful," Katie admitted, shamefaced. "It serves me right, I guess." She explained about the flowers, the snake, the loose boot, and the rolling rock.

Brad sat back on his heels. "You know better

than that," he grumbled, with an exasperated scowl. "You grew up in canyon country." He folded his arms. "You know rock piles are dangerous. Always, when you go anywhere like this, take someone with you. Or at least let somebody know where you are. Never climb unless you're sure of the footing. And wear proper boots."

"I know." Katie gritted her teeth. Did he think she was a complete dummy?

"And now—end of lecture," said Brad, with a shadow of his usual grin. "Do you think you can ride?"

"I think so, if you help me on," Katie replied. She'd do it, somehow, no matter how it hurt.

So they walked the horses slowly out of the canyon.

"Whisper, my darling, my precious Whisper, you saved me," Katie murmured, clinging to the wiry gray mane. "You're so smart, and I love you so much. If I have to leave Rollins and move to the city, I don't know what I'll do. But there's got to be a way for us to be together. I'll find it, if it takes all year."

7

Aunt Harriet and the Double Bar S

"Water—that's all I can see!" exclaimed Allison, flinging herself on Katie's bed and burrowing under the top quilt. She glanced out the windows, lashed by rain. "If I half shut my eyes, I can almost imagine I'm at sea, with waves splashing on the portholes."

"And wind in the rigging," added Katie, huddled in the window seat. At a fresh gust she shivered and wound a blanket more tightly around herself, like a cocoon. "When it blows from the river, this room is really cold." Tully, who had been dozing in his basket, whined and pattered across the floor. "You don't like the wind either, do you? Well, hop up." She made room for him beside her.

Katie was restless these days, for her ankle was indeed broken, and she was on crutches. Every morning Grandad helped her into his aging green Chevrolet and took her to school, where she could manage all her classes except P.E., and in the afternoon the bus made a special loop to bring her home. She spent a great deal of time with Allison, who hadn't yet made other close friends, but even so, she felt imprisoned. Six weeks! She stifled a sigh. Two were gone, but there were still six long, draggy weeks left before she'd be rid of this miserable cast and could ride Whisper. And take a decent bath. Until then she couldn't do anything—not one single thing—about keeping Grandad in Rollins. And her leg itched. And she couldn't scratch it.

"Are you hungry?" she abruptly asked.

"Well—sort of." For once Allison sounded listless, and she followed slowly along as Katie thumped her way downstairs.

Gram was there, placidly working a puzzle. "X—X—" she murmured. "Ancient king of Persia. Xerxes? That fits, anyway." She printed the letters, then glanced up. "Such a long pair of faces I never did see. Rain does that, sometimes."

"We're looking for food," said Katie, as she lifted the lid of the cookie jar. "Empty!"

"Make some popcorn if you'd like," Gram suggested. "Or some more cookies."

Although Katie generally loved to bake, today even the simplest recipe seemed too much trouble.

However, popcorn was easy, and soon, with its friendly crackle and Gram's cheerful face, the girls' spirits rose. By the time they returned to the tower, they felt much better.

"Delicious!" said Allison with a contented sigh, as she wrapped the quilt around her and balanced a bowl of popcorn on her knees.

"BOOM!" The windows rattled and a copy of *Western Horseman* slid off its stack.

"This tower is a little rickety," said Katie ruefully, as she replaced the magazine. "But I still hate to leave it. Allison—I just can't bear to go!"

"I can't bear it either," said Allison. "Now, if we were only mermaids. . . ."

Katie was silent.

"With long flowing hair—and beautiful faces . . . ," Allison said, while Katie patted Tully and looked away.

"We wouldn't have to leave here at all," Allison continued. "We could be new-style mermaids, with an eye for business. We'd supply the Golden Quail with fish—and teach swimming to the P.E. class. We'd—" She broke off. "Katie, is something wrong?"

"Well, sort of." Katie hesitated for a moment, not wanting to talk about it, "Allison, didn't anybody ever tell you about my parents?"

"Not a word." Allison seemed bewildered.

"I guess it's so long ago they don't think about it any more. But I do." With one finger Katie twisted a tuft of Tully's hair, around and around and around, while she told Allison about the storm, her parents' accident, and her own ordeal in the water. "So that's why I'm not exactly crazy about swimming," she ended.

"Katie! I'm so sorry!"

"It's all right. You didn't know." Katie assured her, trying to smile, although her lips felt stiff as cardboard. "I shouldn't mind so much—only—talking about mermaids . . . it brought it all back."

"I'm sorry," Allison murmured again.

Rain still drummed on the windows. *I won't even think about it.* Katie told herself. *I'll just think about Allison, and what fun we have together. I'm so glad she moved in, right next door.*

Allison, who had been noisily crunching the last of her popcorn, set her bowl on the floor. "Chorus is fun," she said. "I'm glad you're singing with me in the pageant."

"It's okay, I guess," Katie replied. She thought a moment. "But no! It isn't okay!" she flared. "I'd lots rather be riding."

"Anybody would." Allison glanced admiringly at the oversize snapshot of Whisper above Katie's dressing table. "My dress is done—bonnet too. My mom finished it last night."

"Mine too, except the hem," Katie replied. "Want to see it? It's right there in the wardrobe."

Opening the mirrored door, Allison took out the

long, blue-checked dress and matching sunbonnet. "Perfect!" she exclaimed, as she held it in front of her and beamed at the reflection.

"I suppose so," Katie said, without much enthusiasm.

"Don't you *like* it?"

"It's all right. I like blue. But when I planned to ride—and my cast will be off just one week too late." Katie could imagine how thrilling it would have been: up and over the hills, in a crowd of mounted schoolmates, with spotlights shining on them, and three covered wagons lumbering along in the rear.

"At least you've got a horse," Allison said. "I've asked my mom and dad for one, and they both said a big fat NO! 'See what happened to Katie,' my mom tells me, every time I bring it up. It doesn't do any good, not one speck of good, to tell her you weren't even riding. She just says, 'If she didn't have that horse, she wouldn't have been there. Now tell me, would you like to have your leg in a cast?' And for once I can't budge her. She's utterly prejudiced."

At this another idea began nagging at Katie. *Allison would love to ride in the pageant.* Resolutely she pushed it down, but it bobbed up again. *Allison could ride Whisper.*

It was like having two people inside her head. *Whisper's my very own horse.*

But Allison's your friend.

If I can't ride Whisper, I don't want anybody to.

She needs the practice. And Allison could handle her.

No! Nobody but me!

Apparently there was only one way to silence the clamor. "Allison!" Katie said it fast, before she could change her mind. "Would you like to ride Whisper in my place?"

"Katie!" Allison dropped the dress. "*Would* I? I thought about it, but didn't want to ask. I'll be careful. I'll do everything—every little tiny thing—just exactly the way you tell me." Her voice rose so high that Tully jumped down and began to bark.

"Will your mom let you?"

"She'll *have* to," Allison answered. "She couldn't say no to that! Besides, she let me take riding lessons in Austria. She just doesn't want to buy one."

"Brad will be there, to help you. And he can bring Whisper along with Britches, for the practices and all." Katie achieved what she was sure was a brave but heartbroken smile. A Kathleen smile. "Whisper can be in it, even if I can't."

So it was arranged. The next day, after school, Grandad took the girls to the Double Bar S, where Allison bounced on the uncomfortable sidesaddle, while Katie watched from an overturned bucket. "You're doing fine. Just fine," she called out. "Don't be scared." She tried to feel generous. *I'm glad Whisper's in it, and Allison, too*, she assured herself. *Of course I am. Only—why can't it be me?*

The sun was warm and the corral fence was knobby against Katie's back. Whisper was so steady now, even with a strange rider, she thought, nothing like the skittish youngster who used to shy at everything, even the sound of wind in the cottonwoods. And it was fun, having Allison here. Next best to riding herself. She was always so full of ideas. What was that crazy one a few days back? Something about mermaids? Katie sat up straight. *We wouldn't have to leave at all! Was that the answer?* Almost forgetting where she was, she tried out the idea, tasted it, like a new recipe. Maybe it would work.

The following Saturday she asked Grandad to take her alone to the ranch. "No, I won't ride," she promised Gram. "I couldn't anyway, with *this*." She gave her cast a thump. "I just want to see Aunt Harriet."

Ever since Katie had come to Rollins as a frightened seven-year-old, she had considered Aunt Harriet her special friend. On that first empty day her aunt had given her a kitten, Blue Boy, and for weeks she had fallen asleep every night with her fingers laced in the soft fur. Aunt Harriet often did something like that—kind, unexpected. She had a no-nonsense way with her, and when her mood was wrong, she could be supremely difficult—prickly, Gram called it—but Katie thought her aunt was special fun. Now, wondering whether this would be one of the porcupine days, she clambered out of Grandad's car and thumped her way into the study, where Aunt Harriet was sitting at an enormous flat-topped desk.

Tall, erect, she had straight dark hair, which she kept severely short, like a sleek cap, because she didn't like fussing with it. Besides working part-time as real estate broker, she ran the ranch with relentless efficiency, and when Katie stopped in the doorway, she looked up, pen in hand.

"Well, Katie," she called out in her deep, almost-harsh voice. "Still dragging your scourge, I see." She nodded toward the cast.

"For ever so long," Katie told her. "They tell me I'll miss it when it's first off, but I can't imagine that."

"Nor I," Aunt Harriet agreed. "However, you'll be good as new in no time." She pointed at a pile of pale green papers. "Want a job? I've nine hundred of these to stuff, and the meeting date's been changed, so they all have to be hand-corrected. Serves me right for having them Xeroxed too soon."

"Of course I'll help. I'd like to." Laying down her crutches, Katie slid into a chair beside the desk. It was always fun to help Aunt Harriet.

"Correct the date. Fold them. Stuff them. And stick on the labels." She dragged a box of books from the corner. "Here. Prop your cast on this."

For a few minutes they worked in silence. "You must be having another big meeting," Katie said.

"We are. And another. And another." A smile quirked the corners of Aunt Harriet's mouth. "People are crazy. Lonnie Evans wants a state park along the river, and somebody else wants to put up a statue of the mayor. Can you imagine Big Jim Andros in bronze? And still another wants to use the city fountain as a war memorial. War! That's right on target, but not in the way they mean!"

"And you keep them all calmed down?"

"I try."

BOOM!

The room shook, a cascade of papers slid onto the floor, and Aunt Harriet calmly gathered them up, saying, "Sounds as if the battlefield had come to us. Door-to-door warfare."

"It was so loud!" Katie gasped.

"I'm well aware of that. They're blasting for the road and railroad, right out there." Aunt Harriet jerked her head toward the window.

In a moment she asked, "And you, Katie? How are you getting along with your encumbrance?" She glanced at the cast.

"Oh, pretty well. My foot doesn't hurt at all now. The only thing that really bothers is not being able to ride Whisper." As if it were a picture unrolling in her mind, Katie seemed to see the hills and the silver-brown river winding far below, with everything big and clean and bright. This was her home, this dry, free land that stretched on and on. Her home, where she was going to stay if she possibly could.

"Aunt Harriet." She waited a moment, for this

was the thing she had come to say, and she wanted to put it just right. "I can't bear to move away, but especially not to a city. I know your business takes a lot of space—but Brad's going to college, so his room will be empty. Could I stay with you? I'd help you, lots, in the house and with the horses too. And—" She stopped, for Aunt Harriet was shaking her head.

"Katie," she said, quite slowly. "We love you, and you're always welcome. But I don't think you've thought this through."

"Yes, I have!" Katie exclaimed. "Thought it through, I mean. Why, I haven't thought about anything else, very much, ever since Grandad told me about it."

Aunt Harriet leaned back and tucked her pen behind her ear. "You say you can't bear to go. Well, no doubt that's the way you feel right now, but lots of young folks change schools. They don't want to, and then pretty soon they like the new one just fine."

Katie opened her mouth, then closed it again, because Aunt Harriet continued talking.

"That's the way it will be for you, too, Katie. You're a survivor. Remember how you got yourself out of the canyon?"

"Whisper got me out. Except for her, I was stuck."

For a moment Aunt Harriet didn't answer. Then she smiled. "You're worried right now, but aren't we all? Part of your trouble is that—that ball and chain."

She waved her hand toward the cast. "It keeps you sitting around and brooding. An invitation to the blues."

"But, Aunt Harriet, Portland isn't just a new *place*. It's a whole new *thing*—a city instead of a town." With one finger Katie began to trace the autographs her friends had written on the cast. "I can't ride in rodeos there, or keep Whisper in training, and she's doing so well."

"True. But you'll find other interests, if you'll let yourself. Remember, even though you can't control what happens, you can control what you do with it. You can reject it—or you can grow."

"Gram said something like that." Katie faltered. "About moving to the cabin. She said it could be an adventure, or a misery."

"And so it can. It's up to you."

"Then, if it's up to me, why can't I turn my life the direction I want and stay with you?"

"Katie . . . Katie." Aunt Harriet's smile had faded. "Sometimes when we get our own way, the price is too high."

"The price?" Surely Aunt Harriet didn't mean she'd charge board! "Well, how much do you have in mind? I know Grandad would pay you. . . ."

"That's not what I meant, and you ought to know it. I mean the price to yourself. Your life has already been torn up once. Are you sure you're ready for another upheaval?"

"Upheaval!" Katie jerked upright. "What do you call this? Having to move to a horrid, straight-jacket city! Going to a great big high school! Not riding any more—anyway, not much!"

"Do you really think that where you live is more important than the people you live with?"

Katie was silent. She wouldn't change her mind. Aunt Harriet could talk and talk and talk, but it wouldn't make one speck of difference.

"Think a minute," Aunt Harriet continued. "Gram and Grandad are your family. Your tie to your parents."

Katie felt her throat growing tight.

Aunt Harriet was speaking gently now, as she used to when Katie first came to Rollins. "What would you do without Gram to lay out the facts for you? Without Grandad to show you the happy side? Who would you find, ever, to be as interested in you as they are? No matter how I tried, I couldn't take their place, and neither could anyone else. You'll be ready to move on someday, Katie, but not yet."

"I'd manage," Katie said. But pictures were again unrolling in her mind. Pictures of Grandad puttering with his rosebushes while he told her stories about her father as a little boy. Helping her with a stubborn math problem. Cooking pancakes for Sunday breakfast. Pictures of Gram making lists and rocking, while they planned a birthday party. Katie tried to close her eyes against the pictures. *Other people will help me*, she stoutly told herself. *I don't need pancakes.*

"And there's another price." Aunt Harriet was talking again. "Have you thought what it would mean to Gram and Grandad to go to a strange city alone, with home and store all in one building? With no young life coming in? Have you thought how they'll feel when you tell them you want to live with somebody else? They love you, Katie. They always will."

"They'd have each other," Katie managed to say, although she felt her face turning hot. *I wasn't thinking about them*, she realized. *I wasn't thinking about anybody except myself. It's just like Brad told me.* And still she wanted so much to stay that she persisted. "Sometimes I'm a lot of trouble. Maybe they wouldn't mind."

"Anything worthwhile is a lot of trouble. But they're happier having you than they would be alone. Besides . . ." Aunt Harriet's voice dropped even lower. "We may not have a ranch for you or your horse either. Your Uncle Steve and I are thinking about selling out and moving to Rollins."

"Aunt Harriet!" Katie's foot in its cast slipped off the box of books and landed with a thud. "You've never said a word about that before!"

"No, I suppose not. Actually, it's a brand-new idea. With everybody else milling around, maybe we just want to join the general chaos."

"Does Grandad know? He didn't tell me."

"Probably not. As I said, we just decided. And of course we may not find a buyer. But you can see it's impossible for you to depend on staying here."

"But—" Suddenly the room, the whole world, looked strange and dark and different, and Katie jumped to her feet, flinging down the leaflet she had been folding. "Doesn't *anybody* care!" she cried. " 'Were moving to town,' you said, all calm and cool. 'We're going to the city,' Grandad said. And I'm supposed to be dragged meekly along like a—a piece of baggage." She folded her arms across her chest. "Well, maybe I'm not a piece of baggage. Maybe I'll make up my own mind."

"Katie, you know we care. All of us do." Aunt Harriet was suddenly stern. "Who drives you out here, time after time? Who lets down your hems? Helps entertain your friends?"

And who gave me a horse? Katie thought in spite of herself. *Who boards it for me, free?*

But Aunt Harriet was still talking. "Would you really expect Grandad and Gram to stay in Rollins, when they can barely make ends meet? Or expect your Uncle Steve to stay on the ranch, just to provide a stall for Whisper? Of course not. However, we'll help you, any way that's halfway reasonable. Have you talked with Gram and Grandad? Told them how you feel?"

"Not very much," said Katie, looking at the floor. She could feel tears trickling down her face.

"I recommend it. A good talk always clears the air. And we won't say anything about this, not to your Uncle Steve, or Brad, or especially Gram and Grandad. Agreed?

"All right," Katie managed to say.

"It's hard enough for them to move away without having us make it worse." Aunt Harriet rummaged in a drawer and handed Katie a Kleenex. "Now, if you'll blow your nose, we'll finish these mailings. Something to do. That's the best cure I know for the doldrums." Pen in hand, she glanced at Katie with an odd little smile. "Still friends?"

"Of course." Trying not to snuffle, Katie sat down.

I should have known, she told herself as she folded a leaflet. *Aunt Harriet isn't soft on herself or anybody else. Not even me.*

Her fingers were clumsy, and the pile of leaflets seemed interminable. Things were worse than she'd ever dreamed. She'd *counted* on the ranch. It had never once entered her head that she'd have to give that up, too.

But Whisper, my darling Whisper, I'll never go away and leave you, she promised. *Maybe Aunt Harriet is right, and Gram and Grandad can help me. I'll talk to them, this very day.*

8

The Last Homecoming

An hour later, with the leaflets corrected and ready to mail, Aunt Harriet took Katie home, and when she came thumping into the kitchen, her grandparents were already having a meal of chicken and baked potatoes.

"I'm sorry!" she exclaimed, as she slipped into her place. "I was helping Aunt Harriet."

"And she needed the boost," Gram replied. "Knowing where you were, we didn't worry."

Katie gave her a grateful smile, although her own worries were still skittering around in her mind. Whisper . . . Portland . . . and hay and oats and a stable. Eating little, she pushed her food around on the plate and tried to think logically, as if she had a sticky problem in math.

First, she had to go to Portland with Grandad

and Gram—that was one of the known factors. Second, she was—yes, she was going to keep Whisper—that was the other factor. *Known? Yes, it's known,* she fiercely told herself. But how was she going to work it out? The only answer was that if she moved to the city—and kept her horse—then she'd have to take her along.

Grandad, as usual, noticed that something was wrong. "Troubles, Kathy-girl?" he asked. "Seems you're pretty quiet."

"Just thinking," she replied, as all her efforts at concocting a grand plan trailed off into forlorn hopes. Well . . . she'd see what they could suggest.

"While I was helping Aunt Harriet, she told me they're selling the ranch. Did you know that?" she asked, rather abruptly.

"Steve just told your grandfather. Can't say I blame them," Gram replied with a sniff. "Harriet never did like ranch life. Time she had a chance at something else." She lowered her voice and glanced sympathetically at Katie. "But I expect you're disappointed."

"Sunk," Katie confessed. "I thought of *course* Whisper could stay there. And now. . . ."

Grandad looked at her from under his bristly white eyebrows. "We've thought about your horse, quite a lot."

"Actually, she's one of the main reasons we hung on as long as we did," added Gram. "We wanted to keep you here, with her."

"Is there any chance you won't go to Portland after all?" Katie hadn't quite given up hope.

Grandad shook his head. "We've been over and over it, and we always come back to the same hard facts. The city pharmacy, with its attached house, is our only solution. I wish we could manage something else—but there it is."

Katie had expected this. "And so, if we move—that is, *when* we move—I'll have to take Whisper along." That much was clear. "But I haven't figured out how. Is there any place at your new store—a barn or something—where she could stay?" *Forlorn plan number one*, she thought.

Grandad shook his head again. "City zoning wouldn't allow it."

"Or could we pay for her to stay somewhere in the city?" Forlorn plan number two.

The long wrinkles up and down the sides of Grandad's face seemed to deepen. "Katie, as we said before, we're on thin ice. We'd pay it if we could, but keeping a horse is sky-high, for folks that live in town."

"That's what I thought." Katie drew a deep breath. "So, I'll have to earn the money myself. The question is—how? And where to keep her?" Plan number three, perhaps not quite so forlorn, but shaky. Very shaky.

"Well . . ." Grandad sounded doubtful. "The

how is tough. Finding a place—not so hard. Our new store is a long way from the center of the city."

"You mean it's outside?"

"Not really. It's in an old suburb, residential, with small acreages and patches of open country not far away."

Country! Acreages! That meant places to ride. *Riding stables!* Suddenly Katie's forlorn plan took a brand-new twist, a dazzling, sure-fire, can't-fail twist.

"Grandad" she exclaimed. "There must be stables around a place like that. Stables need lots of helpers, and I'm good at ranch work. I've cleaned stalls and fed horses and watered them and walked them and helped train them for—oh, for years! I'll get a part-time job! That is . . . I suppose I'd have to have a way to get there. Could you . . . ?"

"That much, Kathy-girl, I could manage. If it isn't too far, and you can earn the money, I'll play trolley car and take you back and forth to your job."

"I won't ask them for money, just Whisper's keep! They'll be sure to hire me on a deal like that! So—Grandad—will you help me find the right stables? Right away? Next week?"

"Not so fast, Kathy-girl!" he commanded with a chuckle. "You're a mile ahead of us already."

"And don't forget your crutches." Gram poured her last cup of tea, tilting the pot far forward and holding its top with one finger. "At the very least, you'd better wait until you can walk straight before you offer to train somebody's horses."

"Well . . . I suppose so," Katie reluctantly agreed. "But *this*"—she thumped her cast—"will be on practically forever."

"Not at all," Grandad assured her. "You'll be fit as a fiddle in a few weeks, and sometime when I go to Portland you can come along and look around." Although he smiled, it was a weak one. "But Kathy-girl, you mustn't get your hopes too high. You're young, and it's a pretty slim chance."

"It's a *good* chance," Katie insisted. "I'd be cheaper than regular help. Somebody's sure to want me." With sudden appetite she tackled her potatoes and chicken.

All through the next weeks, as the autumn sun continued bright and warm, Katie felt as if she were marking time, waiting to go to the city and get a job.

Her heavy cast was exchanged for a walking one, which still itched, but at least she could get around by herself to town and school. She could also help in the drugstore, and thumped eagerly from table to soda fountain to cash register. Five weeks, she counted. Five weeks to freedom, and a chance to find a place for Whisper.

As often as possible she and Allison went to the ranch, generally chauffered by Allison's reluctant mother.

"I'm sure I don't know what's got into Allison," Mrs. Trudeau said one day. "I should think she'd realize, after what happened to you, Katie dear, on that horse—"

"She wasn't on the horse. She had climbed off!" protested Allison.

"Well . . . she rode a horse to get there. And they worry me, horses do." Mrs. Trudeau turned the car into the ranch lane. "They're so big and rambunctious. Yes, even your horse, Katie dear, much as you love it. It's rambunctious."

"Oh, Whisper's a doll," Allison assured her, as the car stopped by the corral. Her mother backed and turned and drove away. "Mom's wavering a little," she continued. "I think she might let me have a horse of my own someday, especially if I'm careful in the pageant. At least she's letting me ride in that." She laughed in her high, clear voice. "She doesn't think anything will happen with Brad close by, and what she calls a 'controlled situation.' "

As they brushed Whisper's gray coat with its faint dapples, the horse gave her breathy little snuffle, then began to nibble Katie's hair. "Are you hungry?" Katie asked with a chuckle. "See how she chews? The stall's all worn there—and there—from when she was young. Once I sprinkled it with pepper, for fear she'd get slivers in her stomach."

She combed a tangle out of Whisper's mane.

"You'll get your carrots all right, but later on," she said. "Allison's going to ride you first. Once you get your treat, you think you're all through."

Allison brought the sidesaddle from the tack room; they cinched it tight and put on the bridle.

But even with the fun of helping Allison ride, even with the studying and working, time dragged. Five weeks were left, then four. The school was busy with plans for the pageant, and the town was stirring, too, getting ready to move.

One day, when Katie and Allison had gone to the store for an after-school Coke, they met a hearse moving at a stately pace, with three private cars following along.

"Did someone die?" Allison asked. "I didn't hear about it."

"They died, all right, but ages ago," Katie replied. "Grandad told me. The cemetery is so low it has to be moved."

"Oh! And your parents, Katie?"

"Not here. They're—in another town." Katie was glad of that.

A few days later, when they were on their way home from school, Katie grasped her friend's arm and exclaimed, "Allison! Look! They've begun already!" A yellow bulldozer was banging its giant claw against a dilapidated building on a side street.

"Katie! What is it?" cried Allison.

"Just a little vacant building. It used to be Martin's shoe store, but they sold out. Allison, this is the first one smashed, but just think . . . it will be happening all the time now! Whenever somebody leaves. Until everything—every single building in town—is either moved away or knocked flat."

They walked timidly past, keeping to the opposite side of the street. A great hole had already been made, exposing broken beams, lath and plaster, festoons of paper flapping in the wind. At a sharper gust a long black streamer floated down.

"I've tried to get used to it," Katie exclaimed. "I've tried not to care so much. But I do care! I do!"

Not wanting to watch, but somehow drawn to it, they stopped across the street from the building. *Crash*! The front door, posts and all, went flat. *Smash-clatter*! With a rattle of glass two windows collapsed, and at the next blow a gaunt brick chimney crumbled, setting up a cloud of red dust.

Suddenly the girls turned away and raced home as fast as Katie could hobble. *It's coming—it's coming*, she thought. *It's not just an idea any more, It's real.*

Three weeks before Katie could shed her cast—Cast Day, she called it—she went to a rodeo at Winters, across the Columbia. Mary Anne won the barrel race, although her time wasn't so fast as it had been at Rollins. *I'd have worked so hard*, Katie thought, watching. *Maybe Whisper could have beaten Scooter.*

The following Saturday, at a very small meet at nearby Rowenfield, one which Mary Anne didn't enter, the times were slow. *I know we could have won here, Whisper and I,* Katie thought. *It's my last year in Rollins, my last chance, and it's all slipping away, just because of that stupid tumble. Why wasn't I careful! I'll never be so dumb again.*

It was late October now, still with clear blue skies, and the poplar leaves were a dazzle of gold. "THE LAST HOMECOMING!" The words were everywhere, on school bulletin boards and posters in store windows, and whenever Katie saw them, she felt a twinge of sadness. The Last Pigskin Queen would reign. The Last Game on the Old Field would be played. But to Katie, the really important thing was that Homecoming meant only one more week until Cast Day. And homecoming was here.

On Saturday morning the mayor opened the cornerstone of the city hall and pulled out the original town plan; a program of the Silver Cornet Band; some Indian-head pennies; a silver dime with a hole in the center, and a menu from the Golden Quail, featuring a steak dinner for twenty cents.

Later that morning several students carried an altimeter, levels, and buckets of paint to a rugged cliff above the Columbia and painted a series of stripes.

"See that red streak? That's the level of the business section, as near as they can measure it," Brad explained to Katie. "That's how high the water will be when it floods the old downtown."

Katie shivered. "And the next one? The green?"

"The grounds of the Congregational church. Right above it, purple is for the Catholic, and orange is the high school. School color, natch. Blue is the Methodist church—same level as your house. And white, away up there, is the water's final level."

Katie gazed in amazement. It was high—so high.

The weekend swept on. The team won its football game; the Homecoming Dance was thronged; and at dusk on Sunday, in the rodeo grounds, the pageant began.

Wearing her long dress and sunbonnet, Katie sat beside Linda in the chorus. She longed to ride, to be out there on the hills, with Whisper. But if she couldn't, she couldn't—and this was fun, too. Who could help being excited on such a night?

Bleachers were ranged along both sides of the arena, the center was clear for close-up scenes, and one end was left open to give a view of the hills, where riders and covered wagons bivouacked, made campfires, danced, and staged a mock battle with Indians. Each time they appeared, Katie strained to see Allison and Whisper.

"There they are!" she said, nudging Linda, as the long row of horses crossed the nearest hill under the searchlights.

"Sure enough. Also my gang—look at them!"

"Big as life," Katie agreed. "Or rather, small as

life." Both little sisters were riding their ponies, close to Jeff on Cherokee. "Don't you wish you and Nutmeg were out there, too?"

"Not a bit! I'd lots rather be right here."

The pageant swept on, telling the history of the area. "Oh, Susannah, don't you cry for me," Katie sang with the rest. And later on, her favorite song,

> "*Away, oh, far away,*
> *Across the wide Mis-sou-ri.*"

Part of the time Katie could hardly sing, because a lump *would* rise in her throat, and tears flood her eyes. It was *her horse* out there, her own Whisper, and somebody else was riding. She knew just how it would feel, the swell of the saddle as Whisper breathed, the furry shoulders, so warm to pat, the tug on the reins as Whisper tried to forge ahead. She'd never again have another chance to ride in a pageant like this one.

Afterward, she found Allison in the crowd that was milling around outside. "Katie! Such fun!" Her cheeks were red with excitement. "I never had such a great time! Never in my whole life! Could you see me?"

"Could I miss you?" Katie said, laughing, for it was impossible to be glum, with Allison so sparkly. "Whisper's light coat really shows up. And you were good, too—really good. You handled her as if you'd ridden sidesaddle for years. I only saw her circle once, even with the spotlights and the crowd." She pulled her collar up to her chin, for the evening had turned cold.

"That was my fault. I let the reins go slack, and just then the band began. Did it look awful?"

"Not at all. Made it more real, if anything. Honest, it was great."

That night, after Katie had gone to bed in her tower room, she lay awake for a long time, thinking about the dam, the town, the pageant. The old song seemed to be singing again in the sound of wind around the eaves.

> "*Away, oh, far away,*
> *Across the wide Mis-sou-ri.*"

She was going away, too, only a hundred miles instead of thousands, but a world away, to a city. Everything would be different there. She would be starting over, facing strangers, beginning a whole new life.

She moved her leg restlessly under the covers. She'd be wearing this horrid, stiff, itchy thing only one more week. Then she could shed it for good and go to Portland and start her search. She would visit every stable there, if she had to. One of them—she was sure of it—would take her on. Soon now, so soon, she would find Whisper a home.

9

Searching

"Poor little town. It looks as if it's been bombed," said Gram, sitting beside Grandad in the green Chevrolet. "There's Mabel Hawkins's house—nothing left but cinders and a big black hole." They passed a pile of smoking rubble. "And Florence Howard's, too. I've played cards in that one many a time, and look at it now." Workmen were swarming over the house inside and out, prying off choice woodwork, while in the front yard two ragged men were sawing up discarded pieces for firewood.

Hurry, please hurry, Grandad, thought Katie, as she riveted her gaze on the back of his neck. But he drove on so slowly that the engine sputtered and jerked.

"Garage sales," said Gram with a sniff, as she

spotted a pair of homemade signs. "It's easy enough to see why folks want to get rid of their junk before they move. But to save me, I can't imagine anyone here buying it."

Grandad chuckled. "You know as well as I do that nobody in their right mind would pass up a bargain."

Please—please hurry! Katie thought again, and at last he turned a corner and started west on the river road.

It was late November, Cast Day had come and gone, Thanksgiving was past, and Katie was started on the long-promised trip to Portland. Her cheeks felt hot, and she hadn't opened the magazine in her lap. At last—at last—she was going to find Whisper a home. And if she failed? Katie firmly put down the thought. She wouldn't fail. She wouldn't even consider anything so horrible.

Picking up speed, Grandad drove smoothly across the old Stone Canyon bridge and on downstream beside the Columbia. The river was brilliant blue in the sun, and the hills on the far side were a dozen shades of brown, with long purple shadows outlining every ravine. Almost at once they passed the dam, white, shining, and so high that workmen walking across the top looked like ants.

From here, the countryside gradually changed, as the hills became mountains, causing the clouds to drop more rain. Instead of dry grass and junipers, they passed long-needled pines, then thick fir forests, where waterfalls tumbled into shiny black pools. One of these was so near the road that Grandad stopped to let Gram see it close up.

"Seems I never get tired of looking," she said with a sigh. "All that water, falling and falling, twenty-four hours a day."

"It's neat," Katie agreed. Generally she hopped out of the car here, to lean against the concrete railing and feel the cold wind blowing from the pool, but today she fidgeted on the prickly seat and willed Grandad to start on. *Hurry. Please hurry. Don't make the trip longer by even a second.* One moment she was sure she'd find just the right job, and the next she was equally sure all the places were filled. How could her grandparents be so interested in the same old waterfall they'd seen a hundred times? She sat back with a sigh of relief when they began to move again.

But at last, after what seemed like the longest ride of Katie's life, the hills drew back, the river widened, and the valley became a broad, flat plain, dotted with houses. Here Grandad turned off the highway and soon pulled up in front of a newly painted white stucco building.

"Here we are!" he exclaimed, stopping the motor. "The new McNeill establishment."

Katie looked curiously at the neighborhood,

which contained rows of neat, low-roofed bungalows and two adjoining stores, grocery and pharmacy—a perfect arrangement to attract customers and also help Grandad with everyday shopping. Hesitantly, she followed her grandparents through the door to meet the present owner, a smiling, bald, slightly plump man with a firm handclasp.

"My wife," Grandad proudly said. "And my granddaughter, Katie. They've come to look things over."

The store was larger than the one in Rollins, with fluorescent ceiling fixtures. *But no jolly round stove*, Katie thought as she walked between the rows of glass counters. *No colored lights or wire-backed chairs.*

"A good many retirees live nearby, so the prescription business is heavy," Grandad explained. "That's one favorable feature. Easy parking is another." He gestured toward the asphalt parking lot. "The cash flow here should be considerably more than we've had before."

"Very nice. Very nice indeed," Gram said, giving her cane an extra thump of approval. They were both smiling as they walked from one area to another. *They like it*, Katie thought with surprise. *They're excited and happy.*

"The food service is more active, too." Grandad stopped beside the high counter where the owner was packaging a pair of sandwiches to be taken out. "All catered, of course. We won't have to do the cooking." He walked on, chuckling.

"You've figured it out really well," Katie agreed. *But* it *isn't Rollins*, she thought. *None of my friends live here. There won't be any rodeos. The only good thing is that Whisper will be nearby*.

One aisle was cluttered with large boxes, some of them opened. "Christmas merchandise," the owner apologized. "Business will be heavy all month."

Grandad looked at Katie and winked.

At the back of the store a door led into the apartment. "So I won't get my feet cold, winter mornings," Grandad said with another chuckle. Because the owner's wife had gone out, they made only a quick trip through the rooms, which, like the store, were clean and bright. Besides the living room, there was a large kitchen with dining space big enough for the precious round table, and at the back were two bedrooms. *But no pantry for Gram's pies*, thought Katie. *No basement. No squeaky stairs—or attic—or colored window panes. It's just a common, dull apartment, like a thousand others.*

"This one will be yours, Kathy-girl," said Grandad, as they stopped in the doorway. To her surprise, it was almost as large as the tower room at home, but long and narrow, pale yellow and white.

"It's really very nice, Grandad," she managed to say, although her voice sounded like a recording. "Very pretty." She was thinking, *But it doesn't have any jigs and jogs—or window seats—or sloping ceilings. I can't look out and see the hills. It's just anybody's room, in anybody's house. It isn't mine at all.*

"Now," said Grandad, leading them to the tiny back room of the store. "We druggists have some things to settle, so that will take a little time. Here's a telephone, Katie, and a directory. Suppose while Little Grandmother gets some rest, you locate some nearby stables. Then when I'm through here we'll drive out and look them over."

"A newspaper?" asked Gram, and soon was contentedly working a puzzle, while Katie jotted down addresses and telephone numbers. By the time Grandad was finished with his business, she had a list of three stables that were close enough for her to get back and forth easily, and four others that were more distant, but still in the same general area.

The first was only a mile away, on a hillside, with sparkling white fences and a roomy barn. The horses in the pasture were sleek and shiny, and the ground of the corral was firm.

If only I could keep Whisper here! Katie thought. *I know she'd be happy*. Entering the barn, which was vast, dim, and warm, she found the owner, a brisk young woman in jeans.

"I'm hoping for a place where I can work for my horse's board," Katie said, trying to sound grown-up and matter-of-fact. "I've had lots of experience on my uncle's ranch. I've owned my horse for three years now and trained her myself to be a barrel racer. She won second in a rodeo." In spite of her efforts, the last words were quavery.

The owner was already shaking her head. "If you could see how long our waiting list is, you'd understand," she said. "We have girls here nearly every day, wanting part-time work."

"Have they—any experience?" Katie asked, swallowing hard. A tall girl walked past, leading a big black gelding who laid his ears back and jerked at the rope. Katie noticed how strong and sure the girl seemed, tapping her whip lightly against her boots, pulling the horse firmly along.

"Let him know you're the boss, Lisa," the owner called out, then turned back to Katie. "If they haven't had experience, they soon get it," she said with a wry smile. "It's a real grind—walking horses, cleaning stables, grooming. We call them 'groomers,' and they take care of two or three horses, every day after school. Some like it. Most of them soon quit."

"Then will you put me on your list?" Katie persisted. "If so many quit, you might come to me pretty soon."

The woman was shaking her head. "I'm sorry—truly I am. But the only girls we take are older than you, by several years I should guess. We don't even consider them if they're younger than sixteen."

"I see." Katie tried to smile.

"You might come again in three or four years." The woman's voice was kind. "I was a kid with a horse once myself, and I know how you feel. But I can't help you right now."

"Well . . . thank you anyway. But I'm afraid three years will be too late."

It was such a perfect place, Katie mourned as she returned to Grandad's car. *Oh well—I've two more chances left.*

However, the next stable on her list was ramshackle and dirty, with barbed wire fences and sagging barn doors. "Don't even bother to stop," she told Grandad. "See how thin those horses are? Their hipbones stick out, and their coats aren't brushed. I could never leave Whisper there."

The next was small, owned by a pleasant, bearded young man who lived in a trailer not far from the barn. "Sorry," he said. "I only take a few horses, and I do all the work."

"Are there any stables around, any at all, that might take me on?" Katie asked him.

The young man shook his head. "There's Bentley's, three miles farther out. It's big, but they use only professional help and lots of machinery for feeding and cleaning stalls. Any place that takes kids would have a waiting list a mile long." He leaned one elbow against the corral fence. "I remember when I was a kid I tried for a stable job and couldn't get one, and it's tougher now."

Katie thanked him, forcing a smile although she was close to tears.

"Anyway, there are four more," she said, as she climbed back into the car.

"Well . . ." Grandad sounded doubtful. "We'll look them over, but they're pretty far out. I could get you to the nearby ones easily enough, but these others. . . ."

"I'll find a way. *Please*, Grandad, take me today, and then if I get a job, I'll figure out the transportation."

However, the results were the same. One by one the owners said they were sorry, but they had no vacancies, or hired older girls. *Much* older. After a long afternoon Katie climbed silently into the back seat for the ride home. Her grand plan had failed.

"How much would board cost?" Grandad asked, turning the starter switch. "Did you find that out?"

"I checked," she managed to say. "It's quite a lot. The cheapest one is nearly two hundred dollars a month."

His face was sober. "I'm sorry, Kathy-girl. We don't have that much margin."

"I know," she replied, gulping. "And I can't earn that much, either. I know a horse is a luxury, and hardly any girls have them, except the ones who live on ranches. Or the town girls who keep their horses somewhere that lets them do the work themselves. That doesn't cost so much." *The lucky ones*, she thought. *I could do that too, if Aunt Harriet would have me*. "It's all right," she mumbled. "I'll live."

But it isn't all right, she told herself as the miles slipped away. *My darling Whisper. Nothing will be the same without you.*

At home that evening Grandad went downtown to the store, while Gram wearily climbed the stairs to bed, and Katie sat alone in the living room with Tully in her lap. The old clock chimed, then struck, and she remembered how Grandad would sometimes let her wind it when she was quite small, with him right there to help. She would pull one chain, and then the other, and watch the shiny pendulum ticking back and forth. It was ticking now. *Tick-tock, Tick-tock. Too-young, Too-Young*, it said.

At a jiggle of the front doorknob, Tully woofed and jumped down, beginning his this-is-my-family waggle. In a moment Grandad walked in and sat beside Katie on the sofa. He was quiet at first, and Tully jumped up again into Katie's lap.

In a moment Grandad cleared his throat. "Life is tough, sometimes," he began in his dry, friendly voice.

"Yes," Katie admitted.

"I'm almost as disappointed as you are about the

stables," he continued. "I was hoping, against all good sense, that you might actually turn up something."

"I'd been counting on it," she confessed. "You told me it was a slim chance, but I was sure you were wrong."

"And I wish I had been."

The clock continued to tick, and Tully closed his eyes with a heavy sigh. "Grandad," Katie began, after a few minutes, "I've tried everything—every single thing I can think of—and nothing works."

He reached for her hand and gave it a pat.

"My only hope now is that maybe Uncle Steve won't sell the ranch after all. Do you think anybody will buy it? If they won't, then do you think he might stay?"

"I think, Kathy-girl, you'd better not bank on that." Grandad's face was sober.

"But he loves it so. Maybe he'll put his price too high, and nobody will pay it."

After hesitating a moment, Grandad cleared his throat and said, "Your Uncle Steve has made up his mind to sell, and chances are he'll do it at whatever price he can. A ranch is an expensive hobby, you know, and with Brad going to college—well, there doesn't seem any need to hang on. Especially since the road and railroad are coming so close. They'll be noisy."

"*Everything's* against me," Katie flared. "The railroad—Uncle Steve, selling his ranch . . . you, moving away. Even Gram—if she weren't sick, you might not have to go." She stopped abruptly. She'd done it again, exploded like a five year old, and it could only make Grandad feel worse than ever. *Why* did she always have to fall apart! "I know you can't help it, any of you. And I love you," she said more softly, giving his hand a squeeze. "I know you're doing the best you can. I shouldn't have yelled like that."

Grandad waited quietly while Tully, in a dream, twitched his paws. The old clock still ticked. *Too-young. Too-young.*

At last Grandad sighed and said, "It's pretty hard to be mad at a dam that doesn't talk back and can't be stopped, but just keeps on growing higher and higher. It's only human to direct our anger against people instead, and the dearest ones are also the handiest ones to blame. So we're angry, and we love them, both at once. That's the way we're made, Kathy-girl—you mustn't be too hard on yourself." He fell silent, and Katie was silent, too.

"This thing that's bothering you isn't just anger. It's partly fear. Strange places, strange schools, strange people—they're pretty scary, especially to somebody who's already had her life turned topsy-turvy.

"I don't feel afraid," Katie mumbled, although a lump in her throat was growing and growing until she could scarcely speak.

After another long silence Grandad said, "You

always were a spunky one." He sounded proud, not sad. When Katie didn't reply, he stood up. "Coming to bed?"

"Pretty soon."

"Goodnight then. We'll still keep trying." He went up to his room, leaving her alone with Tully in her lap.

Then at last tears rolled down her face, and she began to sob. She was weeping for herself, yet not for herself alone. She wept for the river, the canyon, the hills that must be forever changed. For Gram and Grandad and all the other people whose lives were being disrupted. For the shabby little town she loved. For life, which was so confusing.

Even when all her tears were shed, she sat there for a long time in the lamplight and shadows.

10

Old House, Old Town

December came, with cold nights and drifting snow. This was the month for two moves: Katie's, and Allison's.

Since the Trudeaus were to go first, Katie went over on a Saturday to help. "We bought the bedroom set from the owner of this house," Allison told her. "My mom says it's a beauty. And my dad is buying the old desk for his study. The owner is donating the rest to the Salvation Army." She and Katie were heaping clothes into a box to be discarded.

"These too?" asked Katie, holding up a pair of jeans. "They look good to me."

"I know—my mom says they aren't fit to be seen, but I like them." Allison jumped to her feet. "Mom—Mom!" she called, running out of the room with Katie close behind. "Let's take these along. Katie says they look good to her, and I want to wear them till they fall apart."

Mrs. Trudeau, a small, dark-haired woman with a nervous smile, stood up, hand to her back, from a box she was filling with dishes. "But, darling," she protested. "They're in rags. Look at that knee; it's almost worn through."

"They're such a neat, faded color. I really want to keep them, Mom. They *utterly* suit me."

Embarrassed, Katie started back up the stairs, just as Mrs. Trudeau sighed and returned to her packing. "All right, dear. Whatever you say. Just let's get on with the job."

Two days later the moving van lumbered away from the Trudeau door. *It's coming*, thought Katie. *The flood will be here before I know it. And I still haven't found a place for Whisper.*

The next week Katie's family moved to the cabin. This meant farewell to the beloved old house, to the attic and the basement, to the tiny panes of colored glass above the front door, to the bannister she used to slide down, to the hollow in the dining room floor where a dropped item always rolled. To the pantry, where Gram set her fresh-baked pies. To the kitchen, where Grandad loved to play chef.

For the last time she climbed the stairs to her windowed room. Never again could she sit there and look to north, to east, to west—three ways. Never again could she curl up in the window seat, while rain pattered on the pointed roof above.

With a lump in her throat, she marched downstairs, stepping three times on the squeaky tread. "I'll walk," she said to her grandparents, who were waiting in the car.

"It's a long hike, Kathy-girl," Grandad said, but gently.

"Leave her be," said Gram. "I'd like the feel of the good solid earth under my feet, too, if I had the strength. Seems as if I'd want to tramp hard every inch of the way."

With everything washed by the rain, the day was cool and brisk. Although Katie marched swiftly through town with head high and eyes steady, when she came to the river road, tears began to stream down her face. Nobody will notice, out here in the country, she thought, as she plodded along, breathing in jerks and stumbling. Whenever a car passed, she half turned and looked at the side of the road as if searching for something.

By the time she reached the cabin, she was calm again. The movers had already come, so she helped her grandparents direct them where to put things. Most of the furniture fit into the single, very large room on the ground floor, which would be used for kitchen, dining, and living. *It doesn't have any colored window panes,* Katie thought. *Or shimmery chandeliers.*

Her grandparents' bedroom furniture was placed

in the lean-to, which Grandad had had insulated to make it warm enough for Gram. And Katie's own things had to be lugged up stairs that were almost as steep as a ladder. *There's no tower,* she thought. *No window seat. Not even a bookcase.*

Since none of the cabin was plastered, the joists and beams were exposed, dark with time, while the room in the loft had sloping ceilings and heavy timbers. Grandad had had the roof patched and broken window panes replaced, and the house had long ago been given running water and electricity.

"We'll be fine—snug as a bug in a rug!" he exclaimed, when the last piece of furniture was set down and the movers had left.

"I didn't want to come, but it's beautiful," Katie admitted, as she gazed out the window. Uncle Steve's ranch was just across the lane, nestled in tall poplar trees that stood bare against the blue sky. In the other direction, downhill, she could glimpse the new white bridge, and in the distance lay the broad Columbia River, with a rolling line of bare brown mountains on the opposite shore.

Somehow, they managed to find what they needed in the muddle of boxes. Somehow, they made the beds and put together a hasty dinner, using the black iron coal-burning range, because the electric one, perhaps damaged in moving. refused to become even faintly warm. Somehow, worn out by the long hike, Katie slept well, although as she fell asleep she missed the rustle of the cottonwood tree that had rubbed against the house in town.

In the morning Gram crept into the kitchen, white-faced, clinging to the walls for support.

"You did too much yesterday," Grandad said, fussing over her.

"I'll be right again in a jiffy, soon as young Dr. Brady has a chance at me," she insisted, with the tremor in her voice that meant she was in pain.

"Can you manage, Kathy, if we leave you here alone?" Grandad asked.

"I'll be just fine," Katie assured him.

"I don't like to do it. But your grandmother. . . ."

"You've got to take care of her," Katie insisted. "I've been alone before. Besides, Tully will keep me company."

"It's not you I'm worried about. It's the stove," said Grandad with a glance at the range, its coal fire already lighted.

"The Iron Monster?' asked Katie, using the name she had given it last evening. "I watched you work it yesterday."

"Well—all right, then," said Grandad, but doubtfully. "Let me show you how." After telling her how to adjust the controls, he tenderly helped Gram to the car.

At first everything was peaceful. The fire smoldered. Tully snored in his sleep. Katie mixed a cake and put it into the oven.

"Let's see, now. I need a little more heat, and Grandad told me to turn the damper this way. Or was it the other?" she said half aloud as she jiggled the lever. "I wish I'd paid more attention." Checking the stove from time to time, she wandered around, unpacked several boxes, and hung up some of her clothes.

But soon a wisp of smoke curled from the top of the Iron Monster. "So! You'd take advantage of me!" she exclaimed, half in amusement. She rattled a stove lid as she had heard Grandad rattle it last evening and glanced into the oven, where the cake lay flat in its pan, not rising. "Still not hot enough. I suppose it needs more coal," she said to Tully, and poured in half a scuttle full. "And the damper must be wrong—I'll move it back."

At this, drifts, then clouds, then billows of thick, black, sooty smoke eddied from the top of the Iron Monster, making Tully cough, and sending Katie for a glass of water. "Open the windows; I know that much," she said, fumbling at the catch. With fresh air pouring in, she poked the coals and turned the damper handle one way, then the other, but nothing helped.

"Tully, we've got trouble" she exclaimed, as she twisted every lever within sight. The morning "BOOM" rocked the cabin, louder than it had ever sounded in town, and she vaguely realized that clouds of dust boiled up from the new road, close by.

In the midst of the dirt and confusion, she heard the rattle of the doorknob, and Aunt Harriet burst in, sleeves rolled up and a man's jacket around her shoulders. "I saw smoke," she said. "Are you having trouble?" Coughing, she strode across the floor.

"It's the Iron Monster," Katie explained, giddy with relief.

"Iron Monster?" Aunt Harriet darted an amused glance at Katie. "So that's its name! Well, if it's only the stove, that isn't so bad. I was sure the cabin was on fire." Expertly she turned the damper back. "What happened?"

Katie looked at her through the smoke. "I just—I can't find the right handle to turn it off. Grandad told me how, but I guess I didn't listen, and I was trying to bake a cake." She explained about Gram's illness.

"Hm-m." Aunt Harriet lifted a round stove lid and looked into the flames. "Enough coal for a foundry, and choked with ashes." Thrusting a stout, curved handle into a slot at the bottom of the firebox, she shook the stove so vigorously that Tully began to bark. "How come you're here all alone?" she shouted above the rattle.

Katie caught the dog's muzzle in her hand. "It's all right," she soothed him, then turned toward Aunt Harriet. "Grandad didn't want to leave, but he was worried about Gram."

"All this commotion is too much for her, but at

least you're not burning up. Here, I'll show you how to conquer your monster," said Aunt Harriet, and explained the various levers. "You've got enough coal in there for three fires," she finished. "You'll just have to be roasted for a while."

"My cake?"

"Cake?" Aunt Harriet's lips were twitching now.

"It's in the oven. Will it bake?"

"Yes, it'll bake. By now it's probably a cinder." Aunt Harriet held open the oven door, while Katie cautiously extracted the charred concoction.

"Well . . . maybe if I cut off the burned parts . . ." she ventured.

Already the smoke was dwindling, and soon the room was almost clear. "Thank you, Aunt Harriet," Katie murmured. "I don't know what I'd have done without you. Would you like a piece of cake—from the middle, that is?"

"Well . . ." With an amused smile Aunt Harriet eyed the blackened dish. "Not now, Katie. I'll come over later on, to see how Gram is. Maybe a piece then, if you've managed to recycle it."

"I'll ice it, if it's any good. But probably it will be a total loss."

"An astute observation. I'll leave you now, and remember—not too much coal." Throwing the jacket around her shoulders, Aunt Harriet walked briskly away.

In the next few weeks Katie was surprised to find

that she actually enjoyed the cabin, with its dark beams, ladderlike stairway, and low-ceilinged loft. She even became friends with the Iron Monster, which warmed the whole living area. It was fun to sit there with Gram when she first came from school and tell her all about the day.

It was special fun to be living so near the Double Bar S, for she visited it every afternoon. She loved these times alone in the barn, where it smelled of hay and was warm and dim and quiet except for an occasional snuffle or stamp of a hoof. She petted the kittens, which the old gray cat Mindy was tending in an unused manger. She distributed carrots to Britches and Whisper and the other horses, who poked their heads over the ends of their stalls, and Whisper gave her a special, soft whinny, as soon as she came through the door.

"I don't know what I'll do with you," she often said, laying her cheek against Whisper's warm one. "I have to go to the city; there's no way to avoid that. And Uncle Steve wants to sell this ranch." She let the horse's velvety lips gnaw her fingers. "We'll hope he can't find a buyer. Otherwise . . ."

An idea had come to her, although she didn't quite like it. "If I can't figure out a way to keep you for myself—I'll never stop trying, but if I *can't*—then maybe Allison can have you. She thinks her mom is wavering. At least I could see you, lots of times. It would be ever so much better than selling you to a stranger." She mentally filed the idea as a desperate last resort.

By now the town was almost deserted, with most people moved into their new houses, and the work of destruction was going fast. Although Signal Bluff hid Rollins from the cabin, Katie could smell the smoke and see a tinge of blue in the air, and every time she went to school, she passed bulldozers at work.

When Grandad told her that their old home was to be demolished the next day, her heart sank. "I think I'll go watch," she said. "It seems only right to have someone there that loves the house, to watch it die."

"Maybe Allison will go with you," Gram suggested. "They must be wrecking her house tomorrow, too, and bad times are always easier if you're with a friend."

"I'll ask her right now." Katie hurried to the telephone.

The next morning, which was Saturday, she set out on foot, down the hill and across the old bridge. Workmen were getting ready to dynamite it, now that the new road was nearly completed and the old one soon to be abandoned. Main Street seemed untouched, with most stores open, but when she came to the residential district, nothing looked right, for house after house had already been leveled. However, she soon found their own street, their block—and there was Allison, waiting by a tree.

"Rollins looks as if a tornado had come through,"

said Allison, as they walked solemnly along, as far as they were allowed. The old house stood forlorn, with its colored glass and windows gone—sold for salvage, along with most of the fine old woodwork. Gaunt and staring, it seemed to cringe under every blow of the yellow bulldozer, which was already at work.

"There's your room!" cried Allison, as part of the tower caved in with a grinding crunch.

Another crunch and another, and the side wall fell, exposing the framework. Katie saw the stairway, the attic, the closet where she had hung her coats, all open to the air, with wallpaper hanging in streamers. The window seats cracked and split. Stairs dangled cornerwise by a tread.

Farther down the street another bulldozer pushed over a majestic cottonwood tree, which fell with a crash, roots fanning out in the air. Katie began to tremble. "Let's go!" she cried. "I don't want to see any more!"

"Me either!" Clutching hands, they raced away and climbed the hill to Allison's new home, where Katie spent the rest of the morning.

That night, when everyone had gone to bed and the cabin was quiet, Katie felt wakeful. After tossing for what seemed like hours, she dressed and slipped out quietly, so as not to disturb her grandparents. Guided by her flashlight, she followed the short path to the edge of Signal Bluff, from where she could see the town.

The view was eerie. Far to the left, far to the right, the hills loomed, dark rounded shapes with the silver river sliding between them. Near the river, in the old town, was a dull red glow that now and then leaped into flame, for the work of burning went on day and night. That is my town, she thought, and it's being destroyed three times: by crushing, by fire, by flood. As if once weren't enough.

Longing to feel it around her, she left her rock and went down the hill into Old Rollins, to their own now-deserted street. She could sense the empty town stretching out to all sides, windows without glass, black cellar-holes gaping in the moonlight, with all the people gone and the lights turned off. The air stung with smoke. Shadows lurked, and wind whistled at the lonesome chimneys.

Something rustled, and in the moonlight Katie saw a little white dog nosing at the edge of a building. "Here, fellow," she called, holding out her hand. "Are you lost? I am too, in a way. But I'll take you home with me, and tomorrow I'll help you find your family."

Whining, the dog scurried away into the dark. As if he knows what's happening, she thought. As if he's afraid.

Suddenly she turned and ran, away from the fires, away from the wounded houses, away from the town. She alternately ran and walked until she was safely at home in the cabin.

11

The Crazy Eight

"Right there—that's the place. But the branch is still a bit bare. Maybe if you put the light a little farther out . . ."

"Or move this angel?"

"Perfect."

It was late December, and Grandad and Katie, under Gram's firm direction, were trimming the tree. *Our first Christmas—our only Christmas—in the cabin,* Katie thought. She had grown to love it, especially now, with the snow outside so deep and soft and sparkling white, and the Iron Monster keeping the whole house warm. She hummed carols under her breath as she helped Grandad bring in piles of juniper from the hills and unpack the boxes of beloved ornaments.

The day after they put up the tree, Katie had a

Christmas party, the next Saturday she went caroling with the chorus, and on Sunday she rode Whisper to a winter rodeo at the wealthy Fifty-two square Ranch, which had a covered ring. At last—at last, she could race again, and her heart pounded as she fastened bells to the bridle. However, Whisper shook her head so frantically that she took them off at once and substituted a pair of huge red bows.

Once there and well warmed up, Whisper ran her best, stretching out her neck and rounding the barrels with only inches to spare.

"Gram! Grandad! Look! A *blue* ribbon!" Katie exclaimed, when she had returned home and had her horse fed and brushed and blanketed. "Even though Whisper's all out of training. Of course, the others were too, most of them. But she's so young!"

"It's really special," Gram told her, beaming.

"It's also well-deserved," added Grandad.

"And the best part," Katie continued, half out of breath, "was that so many people, cowboys and ranchers and riders, noticed her and said nice things about her. We were—almost famous!"

She proudly pinned the ribbon beside the red rosette on the wall of her room. But she couldn't rid herself of a cobwebby, dark, disturbing thought, for time was rushing past, and she hadn't found Whisper a place to stay.

Christmas morning came at last, with a satisfying pile of presents under the tree.

"I like Christmas around my own table," Gram had insisted, so a turkey was put to roast, and Grandad brought out the holiday china. Just as Katie—wearing her new boots—was rinsing the oversized platter, she heard a rapid pounding and Allison's excited voice.

"Katie! Katie! It's me! Come quick"

When she flung open the door, there stood Allison, bundled to the eyebrows and holding the reins of a brown and white pinto mare.

"Meet Chuck-a-Luck" she exclaimed, patting the horse's muzzle. "Chuck-a-Luck, this is Katie! And oh, Katie, she's my own, my very own. My mom finally changed her mind. At first this morning all my presents were clothes, and I thought, 'What a dumb-dumb Christmas!' And then, when everything was opened, my dad gave me a great big fancy envelope, and inside it said, 'Try the oven.' And it was a *treasure hunt!* You know: 'Now to the schoolhouse door.' 'Go four miles on Winthrop Lane and look in the first mailbox.' And at the end—there was Chuck-a-Luck, waiting for me in the barn of the Big Star Ranch. With a saddle." Allison was too excited for Katie to get in a word. "And I can keep her there, too, and take care of her myself, and ride her every single time I want to. That's part of the present—keeping her there."

Katie was patting Chuck-a-Luck's neck. "She's beautiful, Allison," she said. "So steady and friendly, and such neat markings. How old is she?"

"Five. An utterly perfect age. She's already

learned barrel racing, some, so I can be in the rodeo next summer. Isn't she a *love*!" Allison brushed a tangle out of the horse's mane. "Let's go for a ride, Katie. Hurry. Bundle up, and we'll saddle Whisper."

By now Gram and Grandad were in the doorway, admiring Chuck-a-Luck and urging Katie to go. "Of course you've plenty of time," Gram said. "The turkey's cooking, and the dishes are ready, and your Aunt Harriet is bringing most of the dinner. So run along and have a good ride. Just don't forget to come back in time to eat."

"I'll be here," Katie called out as she flew out the door.

Although it was glorious to have a Christmas ride with Allison, talking about horses all the while, Katie couldn't quite escape a nagging little thought. *It means Allison can't buy Whisper. I'm glad she has Chuck-a-Luck—of course I am. Only . . . what am I going to do now?* She held fast to the thought of Uncle Steve, whose ranch still wasn't sold.

However, a few days later, while she was helping at the store, he sauntered in. "A buyer at last!" he called out as he walked through the door. "He came this morning, and I showed him around, and he's already made an offer. He's letting us keep possession until April, so we can get settled somewhere else. He's—"

Katie didn't hear the rest, because she fled to the

back room. April! she thought. Only three months! Since she couldn't take Whisper to Portland, there was just one thing left. Somehow, somewhere, she'd have to find a place where she could earn the stabling by a summer job. She's have to find it fast.

One by one she considered the ranches she knew. Some were too small, some too far, some owners would surely turn her down. But Mr. Whittaker, on the Crazy Eight, had often petted Whisper and said he was sorry he'd sold her mother. If that was the way he felt, maybe he'd help her out. She'd go see him this very weekend.

She might ask Grandad to take her, but that, she instantly decided, was a horrible thought. Either he'd trail along with her and call her Kathy-girl and try to explain how wonderful she was, or else he'd wait in the car while she trotted in like a little kid who had to be hauled around. The only way she could convince Mr. Whittaker that she was old enough to take care of horses was to handle it by herself. She wouldn't tell Grandad a word about it, or Gram either. Just surprise them when it was all arranged.

The next Saturday she packed a lunch and put on her Christmas boots. "I won't be back until afternoon," she told Gram.

"So long? Won't Allison's mother worry?" Gram was looking over dried beans for soup.

"I'm not riding with Allison," Katie firmly said.

"You're going alone? In this cold? Are you sure that's wise?"

She's thinking about my tumble, Katie realized, and gave her an impulsive hug. "I'll be extra-careful and not take any chances. There's something I want to try. A chance to keep Whisper."

"We'd best talk it over first, before you—" Gram began, but Katie was in a hurry. "Later, Gram—when I get back. Just *trust* me. It's *really* all right." With a wave of her hand, she was out the door.

Although the sun was bright, it was a long ride to the Crazy Eight, so long that Katie's toes began to tingle. Halfway there she passed a lane over which was an arch with a painted brand and name: Rocking C. The Chambers ranch, she thought. It would be fun to ride up the lane and see Linda and get warmed up while they played some tapes. But nothing must interfere with her errand, so she rode steadily past.

By the time she reached the Crazy Eight, her fingers were stiff and ice had formed on Whisper's nose. She dismounted beside the barn, gave the reins to a ranch hand, and found Mr. Whittaker in his tack room.

"Why, Katie!" he exclaimed, when she appeared in the doorway. Motioning her to come in, he quickly closed the door behind her. "I haven't seen you for a coon's age," he continued, big and hearty and kind, in his rough cowboy clothes and plaid mackinaw.

"You're a long way from home. Here, come over by the stove and get warm." He turned up the controls of the electric heater in the corner.

"Oh, thank you," she said, pulling off her gloves. "I've just about turned into an icicle."

"Coffee?" he asked. "It'll warm your gizzard." He nodded toward a battered percolator sitting on the table, with mugs, cream and sugar, and a plate of cookies.

"That's what I need, all right." Katie smiled, thinking this might be easier than she had expected. She curled her fingers around the hot mug, feeling life slowly seep back into them, then tasted the well-sweetened brew.

While she was drinking, Mr. Whittaker inquired about her grandparents. "You don't often come out this way, especially in winter," he said when she had stopped shivering. "Something on your mind?"

"Well, yes, there is. That's why I came." Trying to be brief and businesslike, she told him about the sale of the Double Bar S—which he already knew—and about Grandad's move to Portland—which he also knew—and her need to find a place for Whisper—which didn't surprise him.

"I don't want to sell her," she ended. "But I know you like her, and I thought—hoped—you might keep her here and use her some and let me come summers to earn the rest of her keep." She sat as straight as she could, trying to appear tall and capable—that is, if you could look tall, sitting down. "I know quite a lot about horses," she continued, when he didn't reply. "I've helped on the Double Bar S ever since I came to Rollins, and I'm really pretty strong. I trained Whisper, and I've taken care of her. I'd be willing to do anything you need."

Mr. Whittaker tilted his chair onto two legs and pushed his big hat back on his head. "What does your grandfather think about this plan?" he asked.

Katie blinked. "Grandad? Well, he doesn't know about exactly this." As she saw the tall rancher's eyes beginning to frost over, she realized how strange it must seem to him, that she had come away out here and tried to get a job, without permission. "Both Gram and Grandad were willing to have me work for Whisper's board at a Portland stable, only I couldn't get a job." This was no time for pretending. "I wasn't old enough," she hastily said and gripped the edge of the table. "If they'd let me apply for that, surely they'd let me work for you."

"Do they know you're here?"

"Gram knows I'm *someplace*, trying to do *something*." Katie felt like a balloon with a slow leak. "Of course, I couldn't really work here unless they said it was all right. But I'm sure they'd be willing."

"That's probably true." Mr. Whittaker's face was serious. "I don't doubt that you'd try to earn your keep, and perhaps you could. And your little mare is a good one. Any time you want to make a sale, I'd consider that. But taking you in . . ." His voice was kind, but his eyes were saying no. "Katie, how old are you?"

"Thirteen. Almost fourteen."

He shook his head. "I've enough problems running a ranch without hiring such a young employee. But if you'll talk it over with your grandfather, and let him come to me . . . then, in a few years, when you're older . . ."

"I'm afraid that will be too late. But thank you anyway," said Katie, jumping to her feet. She had to get away fast, before the lump in her throat grew so big she couldn't talk. She'd botched it. She could see that now. She should have gone to Grandad first. But Mr. Whittaker said he'd consider only a sale, so probably it wouldn't have worked, no matter what.

The big man followed her outside and waited beside her while a cowboy brought Whisper, fed and brushed. "I'm really sorry to say no, Katie. I've seen you ride, and I like the way you handle your horse."

"Thank you, Mr. Whittaker," Katie mumbled, as she put her foot into the stirrup. I said that before, she thought. I sound like a broken record.

Mr. Whitaker was still talking. "Now, be sure to let me know if you decide to go ahead with a sale. An outright sale, that is. Whisper would have a good home here. She'd be a ranch horse, of course, but horses like to work. You could rest easy about that."

"I know I could. And I'll think about it," said

Katie as politely as possible, and started toward home.

"Another idea gone wrong," she murmured, as she huddled in the saddle and pulled her scarf almost to her eyes.

Whisper gave a soft little nicker.

"I'm almost glad, in one way, because I don't want you to be a common ranch horse and not have anybody to feed you carrots and keep you nice and shiny. But Whisper—my darling Whisper—nothing is working out for us. And April is coming soon. So soon."

As she jogged along, she remembered the feel of Whisper tugging at the reins in that last barrel race; the softness of her coat when she was a newborn foal; the hopeful way she nosed at her pockets, looking for a carrot. This time, when she passed the lane to the Rocking C, she didn't even want to stop, but jogged swiftly home. There, after giving Whisper an extra measure of oats and a warm rubdown and blanket, she ran into the house.

"It didn't work," she said briefly, in reply to Gram's question.

"I'm sorry." Gram gave her an anxious tell-me-all-about-it look.

But Katie only said, "Anyway, I had a good ride. I'll just have to keep trying. Something is bound to come right."

She didn't tell anyone, not even Allison, where she had gone.

12

Allison

"Saturday again! The time is going so fast!" Katie exclaimed one morning, turning off the vacuum cleaner. "Before we know it, we'll be moving to Portland! And leaving all this." She stopped beside the window to gaze at the snow-swept hills.

"You like living in the cabin better than you expected?" asked Gram, who had just finished dusting the furniture, this being one of her good days.

"It's the most beautiful spot I've ever seen. And it's Rollins." Katie wound the cord and put the cleaner away.

A few minutes later the knocker clanged, and when she opened the door, Allison was outside, holding Chuck-a-Luck by the reins.

"Katie! I hurried as fast as I could. It's snowing again, and the drifts are really deep. But Katie—I've got something utterly wonderful to tell you!" Allison's cheeks were red, eyes sparkling. "You'll never guess. Never in this world!"

"Allison! Whatever . . .? Well, we'll have to take care of Chuck-a-Luck. You can tell me while we rub her down."

"No, I'll wait. It has to have your *full attention.*"

What's up? Katie wondered, as they hurried to the barn. Even when she received Chuck-a-Luck, Allison hadn't been this excited, giggling a mile a minute and refusing to explain. Nothing could be *that* great. But clearly, the only way to find out was to get the job done, so she helped rub down the horse, put on a blanket, and give her some oats.

Back at the house, they pounded upstairs to the loft, where Katie quickly closed the door. "Now!" she exclaimed.

"Now!" echoed Allison, pulling off her jacket and bouncing on the bed. "I've got the greatest news."

"Well, tell me. Quick! Before you explode—and I do, too."

"I've asked my mom, and my dad too, and he left it to her, and at first she said no, but then she said it's all right after all. More than that—they've decided its a *very* good idea!"

"Allison!" Katie was laughing now. "What is this all about? I'm practically expiring to know."

Allison drew a deep breath and sat up straight on the patchwork quilt. "It's this. We want you to stay in Rollins next year and live with us!" Jumping off the bed, she caught Katie by both hands. "And that's not all! You can keep Whisper at the Big Star, along with Chuck-a-Luck. We've already checked it out, and we can take care of both horses together. It's *lots* cheaper that way than a regular stable. So we can ride together all the time. Now, isn't that perfect!"

Rockets seemed to be going off inside Katie's head, and she only stared, unable to speak. Whisper! She could keep her. Rollins High! She could go to school there. Away back somewhere, at the edge of her mind, was a tiny echo of Aunt Harriet's words. *Are you sure you're ready?* But she put it into a little box and resolutely closed the lid.

Tully, who had raced upstairs with them, seemed to have caught Allison's excitement, for he dragged out his tattered sock and sat down in front of Katie, whining between his teeth. "Silly!" she exclaimed, with a catch in her throat, as she held it for him to shake.

"I don't suppose I can bring him along?" she asked, although she could guess the answer.

Allison shook her head and giggled again. "Oh, my goodness no! My mom is still utterly anti-dog. She says they smell! But you'll have me—and I'll have you!"

"And Tully will keep Gram and Grandad company. They'll like that," Katie agreed.

Aunt Harriet's words forced themselves out of

the little box into which Katie had tried to stuff them. *Are you ready? Are you ready?* Maybe she wasn't. Maybe she ought to refuse, straight out. Maybe she ought to say, *Of course I can't go. Thank you, Allison. It's a great idea, only it won't work. I'll never leave Gram and Grandad.*

But she closed the box again and locked it tight. Surely she was old enough to get along on her own, and Gram and Grandad would get along just fine, too. He'd be right there in his store, close enough to help Gram any time she needed it. They wouldn't be lonesome, with each other. She wouldn't think about Grandad making pancakes on Sunday morning, or Gram knitting and rocking, while the good smell of gingerbread drifted from the oven. She'd stay with Allison and go to see her grandparents as often as she could. Every vacation. Sometimes on weekends.

"It's wonderful, Allison," she said. "But of course I'll have to check it out with Gram and Grandad."

"Right away? This minute?"

"Not now. Gram's all alone. I'll wait and ask them both at once. You could stay for lunch, and we'll do it then."

"Okay. I'll help." Allison hopped off the bed, raced downstairs, and started to set the table, talking in excited whispers.

At lunch, Katie was quiet and Allison giggly, while Grandad ate deliberately, chatting with Gram.

"Seems to be something in the wind," he remarked once, sending Allison into a fresh burst of laughter.

They won't care, thought Katie. *They'll have less work with me not there.*

It was Allison who plunged ahead, as soon as Grandad poured his second cup of coffee. "Katie and I have been talking," she said. "You know, we have lots of room in our new house. More than we need for three people. So I got this idea, and my mother thinks it's fine, and my father thinks so, too."

Grandad raised his eyebrows, long and white like banners. *Does he guess?* wondered Katie, as Allison stared at her, lips forming the silent words, "Tell them."

Katie moistened her lips. "Allison has asked me to stay with her instead of moving to Portland. So I won't have to change schools—or leave Whisper—or . . ."

She ran down. Grandad held his cup in midair, while Gram caught her breath in a sound almost like a gasp. "What do *you* think about it?" she asked.

Katie sat and stared.

"What do you want to do, Kathy-girl?" Grandad insisted.

As Allison poked her under the table, smiling and nodding, all of Katie's troublesome thoughts flooded through her mind: Whisper . . . the house . . . school . . . city.

"What do you really want?" Grandad quietly asked.

Katie drew a deep breath. If she said she'd like to go to a stuffy city, that wouldn't be true, and surely they didn't mean for her to lie! And besides, she didn't know how to be a city girl. "What do I want?" she asked. "Well—I like living with you, of course. But also . . ." It came all in a rush. "I-really-do-want-to-keep-Whisper. That's the only way I can." She had a curious feeling that the words didn't fade, but were still in the air, bumping and blundering in all the corners and hovering near the ceiling.

Grandad coughed. "That's understandable. What kind of arrangements would you make?" he asked in a dry, soft voice. "It isn't cheap, you know, to feed an extra mouth. Seems as if they're offering quite a bit."

Katie moistened her lips again, but Allison quickly answered. "My mom wouldn't ask for very much, because she *really* would like having Katie with us, but we thought maybe you would pay a little bit. Just what her food costs, since you wouldn't have to feed her at home. And she can keep Whisper at the same ranch where I keep Chuck-a-Luck. That won't be expensive at all, because we'll take care of the horses ourselves. It isn't very far from town."

"Well, I think perhaps that could be worked out," said Grandad, looking hard at Gram. "What do you think, Little Grandmother?"

"I think Katie is growing up and ought to make up her own mind where she wants to live." Gram hobbled to her rocking chair and picked up her knitting. "But it ought to be understood that it's a trial arrangement only. She's free to come back, any time she changes her mind." The knitting needles flashed, and her chair rocked in quick, sharp little jerks.

"Of course!" exclaimed Allison with a beaming smile.

However, Katie couldn't help seeing the hurt in her grandparents' eyes. "Gram. Grandad. I don't need to go!" she exclaimed. "It was just an idea."

"That's my kindhearted Kathy-girl," Grandad replied with a smile. "But the important thing is for you to do what you want, and be happy about it."

Katie stared at her plate. Why hadn't she told them how much she loved them? Why had she let it sound as if she wanted to stay with Allison? *Because that's what you really do want, that's why*, her inner voice said. *They asked, and you told the truth.* She thought again of Aunt Harriet's crisp, harsh voice. *Your life has already been torn up once. Are you sure you're ready for another upheaval?* But she'd have an upheaval, no matter what. So she'd choose her own.

Grandad was still talking, standing beside Gram now and patting her shoulder with his wrinkled hand that was dotted by small tan spots like freckles. "Little Grandmother and I have known all along that interrupting your school is hard, but we couldn't figure a way around it. And now—here's a way."

All of Katie's problems seemed to be churning around and around inside her head. "It's having our house smashed, and our whole town, and having to leave all the kids. And Whisper." She stopped. Grandad had to leave his store and garden, and Gram had to give up her friends. But Allison was smiling and nodding, and Katie suddenly remembered, as vividly as if she were there, the rodeo smells of popcorn and cowboys and horses, the whinnies and shouts. She could feel Whisper quivering beneath her, ears pricked, eager to run. She *couldn't* go away and never race again.

"I love you both, but I just can't leave Rollins," she said, lifting her chin and looking straight at her grandfather. "I don't want to go to a different school, where I don't know anybody. I don't want to be all cramped up in a city. And there won't be any rodeos in Portland, at least for me. And—" She folded and unfolded her hands, while tears began to run down her cheeks. But she wasn't crying for herself alone. She wept for all of them, whose lives were being shattered.

Grandad fished in his pocket for a handkerchief and handed it over. "It's all right, Kathy-girl. We understand, maybe more than you realize." He smiled at her, his same old, friendly smile. "Now we'll consider it settled and start planning how best to arrange everything. We'll have to talk it over with Allison's parents, of course. When do you girls plan to make the big move?"

"Oh!" Katie sat up straight again, almost hurt at hearing it put like that, so calm and definite, as if it were an ordinary business arrangement. "We haven't thought about that." Smiling a wobbly smile, she handed back Grandad's handkerchief. "I'll stay here with you just as long as I can. Until the very last possible day."

"I'm sure that's very generous of you," said Gram tartly, while Grandad chuckled and said a soothing, "Now, Mother."

"It's wonderful! I'm so glad!" said Allison, giving Gram an impulsive hug. "I'll run along home now and tell my Mom about it."

"Okay," Katie said. "I'll help you with Chuck-a-Luck."

All the rest of the day she was her gentlest, kindest self. A truly Kathleen-person, she thought. She held a skein of yarn for Gram to wind. She made Grandad his favorite cherry cheesecake for dinner. She was careful not to play her tapes too loudly. Although she had a hollow, dark feeling, she fiercely fought it down They had consented right away. They didn't mind too much. And surely she was old enough to manage on her own.

Later, when she explained to Aunt Harriet, she was braced for a scolding, but her aunt only said, "You're sure you've thought it through?"

"Through—and through—and through. I haven't thought about anything else much, ever since Allison asked me. But Gram and Grandad said right away that it was all right. And when he asked me what I really wanted to do, I—well—I told them."

Aunt Harriet sighed. "You're not the only one, Katie, who's having a hard time. There's heartbreak everywhere. I know what people are going through, and I know you're young. Just remember, whatever happens, Gram and Grandad love you. They've shown it today."

"I'll never doubt that," Katie assured her. Dear Grandad. And dear Gram. And dear Aunt Harriet too, for all her prickly ways. Nobody had a better family than hers. She'd make it up to them, some way.

Later that evening she slipped outside and walked through the snowy dark to the barn, where Whisper was standing quietly in her stall. "I don't have to leave you, my darling Whisper Please," Katie murmured, giving the horse an apple.

She put her arms around the warm, satiny neck and buried her face in the mane. "I don't have to sell you to Mr. Whittaker or anybody else. I can keep you after all. Forever and ever and ever."

13

The Last Day of Business

"That will be fifty cents," said Katie. "Yes, that's right, Mrs. Wylam. Only fifty cents."

"And this?" Katie's customer picked up another figurine.

"A dollar. It's a more expensive one, of course."

"I'll take them both." The woman fumbled in her purse. "Such bargains I never did see."

"I know it, Mrs. Wylam. Special prices for a special day." Although Katie smiled as she rang up the sale, her throat felt tight. *The last day—the last day*. Everything she did reminded her that the old store, the old town, were coming to an end, for this was the widely advertised Last Day of Business, at the end of which all the stores in Old Rollins would close their doors for good.

Most of them would reopen later in their new buildings higher up on the hills, but Grandad's would not. "I'll have my final sale along with the rest," he told Katie with a wobbly smile. "The more I dispose of now, the less I'll have to move. Whatever's left after the sale we'll put in storage for a while, until we get possession of our new place."

Already, on this windy Saturday morning in March, the town was full of shoppers, with Brad and Katie both working in the store. Grandad was almost at Katie's elbow, putting a purchase into a plastic bag and talking in his dry, easy way, although she could see that his hands were trembling. When she glanced at Brad, across the room, he grinned and gave her a thumbs-up signal, and a few minutes later she heard him and a little old lady deep in a discussion about the relative merits of cough drops versus syrup.

After a while, when the first rush was over, Brad and Katie found themselves momentarily free. "Suppose I hold the fort here while you buy out the town," he suggested. "Then you can do the same for me."

"Agreed." Feeling oddly excited, as if she were going to a circus or taking a trip, Katie hurried onto the street.

First she went next door to the Sanders Hardware, where she drifted from counter to counter, picking things up and putting them down. In the end she bought a set of bowls.

"Bowls! When Gram already has more than she

can use!" she exclaimed as she paid Mr. Sanders.

Next she drank a Coke at the Golden Quail, while she chatted with the waitresses. At the dry goods store she bought three yards of ribbon, and at Dan's Variety she found a notebook. On and on she continued, up and down the street, in and out the shabby old doors, greeting other shoppers who seemed as aimless as she felt.

I'm doing this for the last time, she thought. *The last time, the last time*. After she had visited all the stores, she returned to Grandad's pharmacy, and Brad went into the town.

"What treasures did you find?" she asked, when he returned with his arms full.

Grinning, he flung down his parcels. "Some pens, a necktie—a *necktie* of all things! And some hair goop. That's the worst. Grandad has a whole shelf of it. But Dan's had it on special, and—" He scooped them into a large paper bag. "Oh, well. It was dirt cheap."

By two o'clock most of the shoppers had drifted away, and those who were left went outside to stand quietly, looking at their watches. The old highway bridge, on the river road, was going to be blown up.

"It's time," Brad said, standing by the door. "They told us two o'clock sharp, and they're usually prompt."

"We'll hear it," Grandad assured him. "Any second now."

BOOM!

"That's it—the biggest bang yet!" exclaimed Katie, as they gazed toward the end of Main Street. Just beyond, past the curve of the first hill, a dust cloud was rising.

"Bye-bye bridge!" said Brad. "That ought to fix it for sure."

Slowly the shoppers drifted back, chatting in shrill, excited voices about the explosion, and where each of them had stood, and how high chunks of concrete had flown, and how large the pieces were.

"Never did see anything like it," said one man, running his hands through his hair. "I wanted to go closer than they'd let us, but when I saw those hunks of cement taking off, I was glad they'd held us back."

A rancher in cowboy boots and big hat agreed. "Thought sure some of them would hit the shoo-fly, but those engineers knew their stuff, and she's still safe." This railroad, elevated over the edge of the Columbia River, was to be used for a few more months.

The rest of the day was busy. Just before six o'clock, Katie, Grandad, and Brad all stepped outside to wait together on the concrete steps. The wind had stopped, and the sun was going down with a brilliant burst of red, like a fire across the sky. Shopkeepers stood in front of their stores and shoppers lined the sidewalks, talking quietly. The hands on the jeweler's clock crept toward the hour. Everyone fell silent.

Oo—oo—oo . . . The town siren began to wail, its eerie lament rising and falling on the crisp air.

"It's over. All over. Forever," Katie murmured, as Grandad and the others simultaneously locked their doors for the last time. Slowly, some blowing their noses, many with tears in their eyes, the people moved along the street to their cars. The Last Day of Business was ended. Old Rollins was dead. Grandad, Katie, and Brad drove quietly home by way of the new high bridge, white, like a butterfly, above Stone River.

But there was still work to be done, so Katie went downtown with Grandad early the next day, to help with the final packing. The store seemed forlorn, its stock skimpy and many shelves bare.

"Packing this up is so sad," Katie remarked, gathering up ceramic figurines and bringing them to Grandad, who was surrounded by boxes and excelsior.

He gazed thoughtfully at her. "I didn't know you cared for it so much."

"I've always loved it. When I was little, it was special fun to come in and see the pretty things. Later I felt important because I could bring my friends to my very own store for ice cream cones. And Christmas! When you had so many lights and candy and toys! There was a doll one year, with a pink dress. I wanted it so much!"

"Did old Santa bring it?" Grandad's eyes were twinkling now.

Katie pulled up a chair beside him. "Christmas morning—there it was! Smiling at me under the tree. Another year, you had some play dishes, and I wanted them, too. Seemed as if I set my heart on everything in sight."

"You were sweet," Grandad said softly. "All eyes and flyaway yellow hair. The *wantingest* little kid I ever saw." He let a wisp of excelsior shower to the floor, unnoticed. "You still are, Kathy-girl."

"I know," she agreed, her throat suddenly tight. "But the things I want now aren't so easy to come by." Swiftly, keeping her eyes averted, she handed him bunches of excelsior to stuff into the boxes. "Summer was nice, too. The trees by Bone Creek Ravine were so pretty, and it was always cool in here—anyway, cooler than most places—and the old chairs and table, with their curly legs, were fun to climb on."

"They've been here a long time," Grandad said. "Ever since my father kept the store, when I was a boy. He had these chairs even then, and I always thought they were special."

"The whole store is special," murmured Katie. "I wish we could keep everything just the way it's always been."

Grandad sat very still, hands full of excelsior. "Things always change. Much as we'd like to, we can't go back. We've got to keep our faces forward."

"But losing our whole town seems—well—it's more forward than I want to face."

Grandad shook his head. "You know, Kathy, it isn't here only that towns are being swallowed. It's happened in lots of other places, too, and it will happen again. Dams are still being built. Acres of concrete smother the fields. Towns grow on what were farms. Some call it progress."

"Is it progress?"

"Well, that depends." Grandad was almost whispering. "I guess only time will tell."

Katie brushed back her hair. "I don't like it," she said, and soberly continued packing until Grandad told her it was time to stop.

14

The Trestle

Spring continued cold and windy until April, when warm weather came in a rush, along with a relentless gray drizzle that poured from the gray sky. Newscasters announced that all records had been broken. The snow pack, which was unusually heavy, shrank back toward the peaks, causing streams to rise until many of them spilled over their banks.

For days on end Gram didn't leave the cabin. "I'm housebound for sure," she said, staring at the spidery streaks of rain on the window. Her knitting and crosswords lay untouched.

That evening, just as they finished dinner, she had a telephone call. "Bless you!" Katie heard her say. "It will be like getting out of jail."

Beaming, she set down the receiver. "It was Harriet," she told Grandad. "She invited us to a meeting in the high school auditorium. Of course, it's wretched weather for a trip to town, but we'll bundle up, and she said they'd deliver us door-to-door. Brad's riding in with us—debate team, I think—and Steve's going too. We'll be well looked after." She began to hobble around, collecting her umbrella and wraps.

"A meeting?" Katie asked. "What meeting, for goodness sakes, on a night like this?"

Gram chuckled. "One of Harriet's interminable committees, making a public report. She said it wouldn't be very late. Katie, you'll be alone, and if it storms again—"

"I'll be okay. Lots to do," Katie assured her, as she settled down at the round table with her Spanish book. Verbs! Not exactly her favorite topic. But she might as well get started and have it over.

With Grandad and Gram gone, the cabin was silent—and yet it wasn't, quite. It was full of old-house creaks and sighs; wind whistled around the corners, and soon the rain began again, hurling sheets of water against the windows.

"This is almost scary," Katie told Tully, who was drowsing at her feet. She put more coal into the Iron Monster and moved to the side of the table that was closest to its cheerful glow.

In another moment she heard the deafening rattle of hail, and when she looked out, she saw the ground already glistening with ice. *At least*, she thought, *this waited until Grandad and the others could get to their meeting*. While she was watching, the hail stopped, as suddenly as it had begun, and she again tackled the Spanish verbs.

"*Caigo*, *cais*, *cae*," she recited aloud to Tully, who was jerking in his sleep. "*Quepo*, *cabes*, *cabe*." Deciding to make some popcorn, she dropped to her knees beside the lowest cupboard, where the popper was stored.

BOO-OO-RR-OOM! It was a rending, tearing crash as loud as thunder, but more jagged and sharp.

"Tully! A tree must have blown down!" Katie exclaimed, and the little dog awoke with a jerk. "But it was so loud! I'd better have a look." She pulled on her heaviest parka and tied the hood.

Outside, gasping in the wind, she counted the trees. Two . . . three . . . four. They were all there. The barn? It was standing, too, barely visible through the dark. A car gone off the road? Darting back into the house, Katie pulled on rubber boots.

"No, Tully, not this time," she said, as she picked up a flashlight and hurried outside again, taking her gloves out of the jacket pocket.

The air had the peculiar muddy smell that comes with high water; hailstones were slippery underfoot, and the night had turned so cold that Katie felt chilled even through the down of her jacket. As she slogged along, she flashed her light from side to side, feeling rather like the heroine of a western movie. "She struck boldly into the night," she murmured, "where nobody else dared to go. Unafraid, tireless, she—"

"She didn't find a thing!" she ended wryly when she reached the road, for everything there seemed normal, with no tire tracks going over the side, no broken guard rail. Had the sound come from the other side of Stone River? She'd better look there, too.

Confidently, Katie started across the bridge, the high, white bridge like a butterfly. But she stopped, for it was quivering, as a torrent rushed through the canyon with a deafening roar, and hurled boulders against the supports. Remembering the storm so long ago, and the terror she had felt then, Katie wanted only to flee back to the house.

Kathleen—no, Kate—do your duty, she sternly told herself, and shut out the memory. But the bridge—had it always been so shaky? The roadway—did it always slant downhill? Walking slowly, because it was slick with hail, Katie trained her light on the road ahead.

It sagged.

It sagged more.

And—

Her foot slipped. Falling, she began to slide, and as she looked ahead, she saw that the roadbed bent down and down, to end in a black void. The center of the bridge had been washed out. She was skidding toward the gap.

Frantically, she clawed with both hands and dug her heels against the slippery hail, scraping, sliding, twisting. Although she couldn't stop, she did manage to skitter sidewise until, almost at the broken end, she bumped to a halt against the concrete railing. There she clung for several long seconds, as she fought for courage to make her way up that treacherous slope.

She had to get help. Terrified as she was, she was able to think that far. Cars would be coming along. Gram and the rest would come as soon as the meeting was over. She had to get to a telephone, or they would drive over the end.

Trembling, keeping close to the concrete guard rail, she crept on hands and knees, inch by painful inch up the perilous incline, where one careless move would start her sliding again. When it leveled off at last, she stood up and ran toward the house over the slippery hail, falling, jumping up, racing on, until she burst through the door and dashed to the telephone.

It was dead. *Of course*, she thought. The line came across the bridge. It was lucky the new electric wires were strung from high towers set on solid ground, or the lights would be gone, too.

Trying to keep calm, Katie spoke to Tully, who was watching her with his head cocked to one side. "There's only me to do something," she told him. "Nobody else knows what happened."

Tully waggled his ears.

"I've got to get help," she continued, while Tully continued to watch, black eyes glittering behind his fringe of hair. "But how? Nobody's at Uncle Steve's. There aren't any close neighbors on this side of Stone River."

Tully woofed, while Katie tried to think sensibly. Even if she saddled Whisper and found a rancher, away off somewhere, what good would that do? With the telephone out, nobody on this side of the river could call the town, and with the bridge out, they couldn't get there, either.

"In other words, it's up to me to get across. Somehow."

Katie could feel her mind running around and around, like a mouse in a maze. The telephone . . . the bridge . . . Whisper . . . the bridge . . . a car . . . a train . . . the trestle. THE TRESTLE!

"That's it!" she shouted, dashing into the kitchen, while Tully ran for his sock. Lanterns at this end of the bridge would stop cars here. The railroad trestle would take her across the river—unless it was washed out, too.

Clutching her flashlight, she hurtled out the door and raced to the barn. There she dragged two kerosene lanterns from their shelf and sloshed them back and forth. They were full enough, and with trembling hands she put matches to the wicks. They caught. Burned with a steady flame. It was a good thing Brad had taught her that, long ago. Passing Whisper's stall, she gave her a quick pat on the nose, then plunged into the night.

The wind howled, shrieked, and snatched her breath. She squished into mud, skidded on the hail. At the highway she set down the lanterns, which made this end of the bridge safe. Then, guided by her flashlight, she slipped and slid down the rocky slope.

She fell and scraped her knees. Got up and floundered on. By the time she reached the railroad tracks she was breathing fast, but the cindery roadbed was level, and she soon came to the trestle. There, in the yellow beam from her flashlight, she could see the steel rails going on, straight and shining, until they vanished into darkness. Below her, the river was loud, like the roll of thunder, as it swept through its gorge and tumbled boulders that Katie knew might be as large as trucks.

Pausing long enough to clip her flashlight to her belt, she moved cautiously to the edge. Now she would have to crawl along the rails, from one tie to the next, with open spaces between. *I can't do it*, she thought, horrified at the gaps between ties. *I'll fall through. The holes are bigger than I am.* Again she was engulfed by the terrifying memory of cold water, wind and waves, and the lonely months afterward of longing for her parents, only half understanding what had happened.

And now Grandad and Gram were in danger. She had to get across—fast—before they started home.

Trembling, she dropped to her knees, crept onto the first tie, and took hold of a rail. Coated with ice, it stung her fingers, even through the heavy gloves. Wind whistled, freezing rain beat in her face, and far below her the roaring stream banged rocks and trees against the girders, shaking them with every crash. The ties were an arm-length apart—far enough for her to slip through unless she got a good hold. "I can't do it," she said aloud, her voice lost in the roaring storm. "I can't—but I've got to." Somehow she kept on, dragging from one tie to the next, afraid to look down, while the flashlight at her belt kept getting caught. One moment of carelessness would plunge her headlong into the torrent beneath.

"Gram . . . Grandad . . . be safe. Don't start for home. Wait until I get across," she murmured, over and over. Here was another empty space. She almost slipped, and screamed. But she reached again and crossed the gap. Tie after tie she pressed on, until she felt the scratch of cinders under her hand and knew she was on the other side.

For a moment she lay flat on good solid earth and tried to catch her breath. Then, jumping to her feet, she ran to the highway, where she turned toward Rollins and stumbled forward as fast as she could. If another car came now, she could warn it with her flashlight. The lanterns would stop cars on the other side. So—she'd made it. If only someone hadn't already driven over the edge. If only Grandad and Gram . . . and Aunt Harriet . . . and Uncle Steve . . . and Brad . . .

She plunged wildly ahead in her heavy boots, shining her light and pulling her free hand into its sleeve, for the wind was cold. At the driveway to the first ranch she propped the flashlight on the road, to stop any cars that might come along, then raced to the house.

"Help!" she screamed, banging the door with all her might. "Help me! The bridge is washed out."

Almost at once the porch light snapped on, and Ralph Newberry, a rancher she knew slightly, appeared in the doorway.

"Trouble?" he asked, and even before Katie finished explaining, he was pulling on a jacket and gloves. "I'll get lanterns," he said.

His wife had come to the door, too, and three wide-eyed little boys.

"Get on the phone," the rancher told her. "Get the state police. Fast as you can." He dashed down the porch steps and was gone.

Katie followed Mrs. Newberry inside, but this phone was dead, too, and they returned to the porch.

"Never mind," said the rancher, reappearing with two lanterns. "I'll hightail it into town."

"There's a meeting—my grandad and gram are there. They might start for home any time now."

"I'll check on them." He was gone in a rush.

"It's all right," said his wife, leading Katie again into the house. "Ralph will put lanterns on the road and get help. You've done your part. And goodness . . . your knees!" She examined Katie's torn jeans, bloody around the edges. "How did you get here, anyway?"

"By the trestle," Katie explained.

The biggest boy whistled. "Wow! That's scary, even in the daytime! I've—" He stopped, for his mother was shaking her head. "I'm not supposed to climb on it at all," he amended. "Were you scared?"

"Out of my skin," Katie confessed.

Gratefully, she sat back in a chair while Mrs. Newberry washed her knees and bandaged them and made a steaming mug of chocolate.

An hour later the rancher returned to report that the meeting had been ready to break up when he got there, but nobody had yet left: That apparently no one had gone over the bridge because so few cars were out on such a night. That all the people who lived on the far side of Stone River would be put up overnight in town. And that, yes, Gram and Grandad, Aunt Harriet and Uncle Steve—they were all safe. "I saw them and talked to them," he finished, "and you're to stay here until morning."

As Katie sank into the smooth sheets, she was swept with joy.

However, she lay awake for a long time, remembering the roar of the river, the crunch of debris, and the wind. Hard as she tried to go to sleep, she recalled every moment, over and over, until it seemed as if she would never get off the trestle.

She'd been so scared, too scared to do it. But she did. She'd started—and kept on going—from one tie to the next, until she got across.

In spite of herself, pictures kept unrolling in her mind, pictures of Gram and Grandad plunging over the broken end of the bridge, of Uncle Steve's station wagon spinning end over end. She tried not to think, and still the images crowded past: images of living forever without Gram and her rocker and cane and puzzles; without Grandad and his garden. At last she began to cry, and wept until the pillow was soggy.

My family, the most important thing in the world! she thought, as she burrowed under the quilt. *Nothing else matters. But I had to almost lose them to find it out.*

15

Time of Decision

By morning the storm had settled into a steady rain, which lashed the sodden ground and drummed on the windows. Mrs. Newberry had washed her jeans, and Katie insisted on going to school, where she was surrounded at every break between classes. Her teachers, friends, and even students she barely knew wanted to hear all the details of the crash, the bridge, and crossing the trestle. Reporters from the *Rollins News* and the *Portland Oregonian* interviewed her. The principal called her into his office to say that everyone was proud of her, and he took her to a doctor who assured them that her knee was only bruised.

At the end of the P.E. class, which Katie sat out because of her stiff knee, she managed to draw Allison into a corner of the locker room. "Allison," she said, "I've got to tell you something. I don't think you'll like it much."

"I will—I will," Allison said. "Anything you say or do is okay, after last night. You were heroic. Utterly noble."

"But this—it's a big change, for both of us."

Allison dropped down on a bench and sat quietly with Katie beside her.

"I learned a lot yesterday," Katie began, longing to explain it just right, so Allison would understand. "When I thought Gram and Grandad might have driven off the end of the bridge, all I could think about was how wonderful they've always been to me." She was clasping and unclasping her hands. "They're my family, and I need—I *want* to be with them, more than anything else in the world." She remembered a time when she was sick and Gram sat right there hour after hour beside her bed, not talking much, just knitting—comfortable, soothing. "So, Allison—you're my best friend, but I can't stay with you after all."

"They said it would be all right." Allison's voice sounded odd, as if something were strangling her.

"All right—yes. But it's not what they'd really like. And not what I'd like, either."

"You don't want to?"

As Katie stared at the floor, it almost seemed as if Stone River were there, roaring beneath her. Again, in her mind, she edged her way across the trestle; again she felt the terrible fear that her family might be lost. "I'd *like* to live with you," she said, struggling to make it clear to Allison, and to herself too. "But what I really want most of all is to be with Gram and Grandad. And the biggest reason that I wasn't going with them was because I was afraid."

"Afraid?"

"Afraid of the town and the school and especially of the kids there. Maybe they like different things than I do. They might wear different clothes. Maybe I won't fit in."

"And now . . . ?"

"Allison, when I crawled across that trestle, I found out that I can do anything I have to, no matter how hard it is. Because I was just about scared enough to die."

"Anybody would be."

"And I got across, just the same." Katie drew a deep breath. "I know now that I'm the boss of myself. Moving to a city will be hard, but I can do it. I couldn't be really, truly happy any other way."

"And Whisper? What about her?"

Suddenly everything was blurry—the benches, the door, the windows. For a moment Katie closed her eyes, and when she opened them, she answered in a voice that quivered in spite of all she could do. "I can't keep her. There's no way, none at all."

Allison began to put on her socks, inching them

over her toes and heels, smoothing every wrinkle. At last she said, "I knew it was too good to be true. But it would have been such fun."

"I know. It seemed just about perfect." Katie managed a smile. "But at least we can get together for weekends, or spring vacation. Maybe I can come for the rodeo and watch you ride Chuck-a-Luck and win a ribbon." *I won't be riding. It won't be the same*, she thought. *I'll be sitting in the bleachers, watching everybody else.* The old feelings swept over her again—*it isn't fair*—but she fought them down. *This is what I want most of all to do*, she told herself.

"Can you, maybe, understand?" she asked aloud.

When Allison replied, her lips were not quite steady. "I'll try, anyway. Of course you have to do what's right."

"And we're still friends?"

"Always." They left the gym together.

Although Katie had seen Grandad and Gram early in the morning, there had been time for only a quick hug, and she knew Uncle Steve had taken them home by the long route upstream, along Stone River, then across a distant bridge. Now the school bus followed the same road, with Katie impatiently watching every twist and turn.

By the time the bus pulled up at their lane, the rain was over, and sunset glowed in billowy pink clouds all across the sky. Bounding down its steps as fast as her stiff knee would let her, Katie hurried through the door, calling, "Gram! Grandad!"

As she rushed into the main room, Gram struggled to her feet. "Katie! Let me feel all your arms and legs. Seems as if I've got to make sure you're really all right."

"Oh, I'm fine, except I hobble, sort of," said Katie, returning her hug.

Grandad was there, too, reaching for her hand. "Katie, we're so proud of you. We—" He broke off, but gripped her fingers so hard they hurt.

"Oh . . . well . . ." She mumbled "I just started out and kept going. There wasn't anything else to do." Flinging off her jacket, she stood by the Iron Monster to warm her hands. She wanted to say the next thing just right, and she wanted to say it fast. "Gram, Grandad—I've changed my mind. I'm not going to stay with Allison after all."

"You're—What did you say?" Gram stopped beside her rocker, resting her hand on its high back.

"I'm going to Portland with you."

A trace of Gram's old tartness returned. "Not from a sense of duty, I hope," she said.

"Not one bit," Katie replied. "I've been thinking, all day and last night too, about a lot of things. When I was out there on the trestle—" She paused.

"You grew up a notch, didn't you, Kathy-girl," murmured Grandad.

Katie gazed into his mild blue eyes. "A great big notch," she agreed. "I was just about scared to pieces, but I got across—and now it seems as if I'm not afraid of anything."

"Not even of the new school?" asked Gram.

"Not even of that."

Grandad was looking oddly at her. "You still haven't answered the most important question. Why have you changed your mind? A matter of courage only?"

"Only part," said Katie, feeling as if she would cry. "Mostly it's because I want to. I found that out on the trestle, too."

"Then that's all right." Grandad smiled and patted her shoulder. "We'll be right glad to have you, Kathy-girl."

"I'm glad you're glad," said Katie, feeling as if a light had suddenly gone on. "But now I've got a horse to feed." She slipped into her ranch jacket, took a bunch of carrots from the refrigerator, and limped out to the barn, where Whisper nickered softly as she came through the door.

"Here's a treat." Katie held out a carrot, and another. In the warm, quiet barn, with Whisper so close, she realized more fully what she had just decided. "I can't keep you after all," she murmured, as for the first time in the whole long day she let the tears roll down her face. She could cry here, and it wouldn't matter. "There's no way. I've tried everything, and none of it works. You'll have to go to Mr. Whittaker's ranch."

She thought of all the years with Whisper: the frisky little foal swishing her brushy tail; the long-legged yearling, nosing into a bucket of oats; the full-grown mare, running her first race. The shouts of the crowd. The shine of the red rosette. She kissed the bristly forehead, ran her fingers through the forelock, rubbed the silky hollow place behind Whisper's ear. "I can't even think of a better place to sell you," she said. "The girls in town either have a horse, or they don't want one, and the girls on ranches already have more than they can ride."

Whisper nickered under her breath.

"More carrots?" Katie asked. "Silly, you've eaten them all." She began to stroke the furry shoulder. "They'll be good to you on the Crazy Eight. Otherwise I wouldn't let you go. And you'll like being a ranch horse, I think. Anyway, Mr. Whittaker said you would. Maybe you can still be a barrel racer and prove how wonderful you are. But we've only a few weeks left." Winding her arms around the horse's neck, she buried her face in the scratchy mane.

Two days later, on Saturday, she brushed Whisper with extra care, put on the saddle, and rode back from the Columbia River, up and up into the hilly ranch country. She hadn't told anyone her plan, not even her grandparents. There was no use to worry them, and this was something she was sure she could do by herself, because she'd already talked it over with Mr. Whittaker.

The day was warm, and in the sunshine the hills were brilliant with daisies and purple lupine. As Katie jogged along, she remembered the last time she had ridden this road, and how hopeful she had been then. "I was looking for a place for us both," she said to Whisper. "Now, it's just for you."

Whisper snuffled and tossed her head.

As she drew near the Rocking C Ranch, Linda's ranch, which Katie had so often visited, she thought that never again—never, never again—would she come clop-clopping along this road, breathing the good sharp smell of sagebrush and dust. She'd hurry on and try not to think about it.

However, just as she passed the entrance arch, she saw Linda's two little sisters riding down the ranch lane on their ponies, and she pulled to a halt. "Hello!" she called. "I haven't seen you for ages."

"Katie!" exclaimed the older one, Stacey, and the two stopped just under the arch. Stacey was round-faced like Linda, with braids and freckles. "Are you coming to our house?"

"Well—not this time."

Both little girls were watching her with wide brown eyes. "Katie," Stacey continued, "Linda told us what you did. Were you scared?"

"Pretty scared," Katie admitted.

"Did you hurt your knee very much?"

"Not very. It'll be well in a few days."

"That's a nice horse," Stacey continued, while the younger girl only smiled. "Linda told me what a good racer she is, and I saw her run, once."

"Well, yes, she is good," Katie agreed. Suddenly she noticed Stacey, on her pony, seemed to be all arms and legs. "You're getting so tall!" Katie exclaimed.

"I know," the child replied, sitting up straighter in the saddle. "I'll be in the sixth grade next year."

"Almost in junior high!" Even as Katie said it, an idea dawned. "I think I'll go up to your ranch," she said. "Want to come along?"

"We can't." Stacey replied. "We're going to the Circle K for the day. But Katie, Linda isn't there. She and our mom went to town."

"That's all right. It's your dad I'm going to see." Katie wanted to break away as fast as she could. " 'Bye now. Have fun, and I'll talk to you again sometime." With a quick wave, she cantered up the lane.

The Rocking C was a large ranch, its rambling house almost surrounded by poplar trees. Although no one answered Katie's knock, she soon found Mr. Chambers beside the garage, working on the engine of a blue truck. He stood up, wrench in hand, when she approached.

"Katie! You're a long way from home!" His mouth widened in a grin as he held up his greasy hands. "Afraid I'm not fit to shake."

"That's all right. I just stopped by—"

"To see Linda? She's gone to town. To the dentist, as usual."

"Actually, I was looking for you." Katie bravely came straight to the point. "It's about my horse."

"Oh—well." Mr. Chambers tossed the wrench to the ground, turned off the engine, and wiped his hands on a large blue rag. In the sudden stillness Katie could hear the call of a meadowlark, full and round, like a bell.

"What can I do for you, Katie?" Mr. Chambers asked.

Katie tried to smile. "You see, she's really a very good horse. And she's used to girl riders, because I've had her ever since she was a tiny little foal, and I trained her myself." She thought of Whisper on her spindly little legs, following her around the corral, nosing at her pockets.

Mr. Chambers stood quietly, wiping his hands, finger by finger.

"And she's a good racer, too. She won first place at the Christmas rodeo."

"I was there," Mr. Chambers reminded her. "Splendid race."

Katie picked a burr out of Whisper's mane. "You see, I have to sell her," she said, "because I'm going to Portland. And I met Stacey at the end of the lane. She's getting so tall!"

"I know." Mr. Chambers chuckled. "Growing like a weed."

"So I thought—" Katie stopped. How could she do it, offer her dear, her darling Whisper for sale? "She really is a good racer. Lots of people have told me so. Just right for Stacey. And I wouldn't ask too high a price, if she could have a good home."

The rancher folded his arms across his chest. "Katie, are you trying to sell me your horse?" he asked.

"Yes. *Please* buy her, Mr. Chambers. So she can still be in rodeos. So she can be special to Stacey. She's used to being talked to a lot. And having carrots. And she's gentle—"

"Well, now," said Mr. Chambers, patting Whisper on the shoulder, "I've known her for some time, and I'm sure she's a fine animal. Steady. Smart. Good-tempered. And it's true, Stacey is going to need a bigger mount pretty soon." He ran his hand along Whisper's foreleg. "I intended to pick out a yearling and get it trained for her. Maybe you have a good idea there. Might save me a lot of trouble."

"And she'd be a barrel racer?"

He laughed. "What else? Stacey's different from Linda. Talks about rodeos in her sleep. Whisper would have her chance, don't worry, and win the Rocking C some ribbons, too." He looked sharply at Katie. "What do your grandparents think about this?"

"I haven't told them," Katie confessed. "I just got the idea. But I know they'll say it's okay. They realize I can't keep her."

"I think so, too—only you really ought to check it out." Mr. Chambers stood beside Whisper's head, stroking her nose. "You've got a price in mind?"

"Just whatever is fair."

Katie heard the meadowlark again, while Linda's father stood lost in thought. In a moment he named a price, larger than she would have guessed. "Does that sound fair to you?" he asked.

"It sounds just fine." It would have been okay, whatever he said, she told herself. Having her horse in a good home was what really mattered.

Whisper stood quietly, shivering her skin now and then against a fly, while Katie and Mr. Chambers talked over their plans. He agreed to see Grandad the following week, to complete the sale.

"Thank you, Mr. Chambers," she said, as calmly as she could, when the lump in her throat was growing and growing and threatening to strangle her. "And goodbye now. I'll tell Grandad you're coming." She managed a wavery smile as she mounted and gathered up the reins.

However, Mr. Chambers grasped the bridle and held her back. "Katie, I know it's hard to give up a horse," he said. "I've made some sales myself that nearly broke my heart. But you won't entirely lose track of her. Linda will want you to visit us, any time you can. You can ride Whisper then."

"I'd like that," Katie replied, as she slipped her

feet into the stirrups and picked up the reins. With a wave of her free hand, she started down the lane.

Whisper's hooves plopped into the soft road as she trotted steadily along under the weak spring sun.

"Whisper, my darling Whisper. You can be a barrel racer after all," Katie murmured, combing her fingers through the mane. "We can't do it together, but you'll have somebody to love you and feed you carrots, and lots of other horses to run with. You'll like living here."

"Whuff-ff," said Whisper, tossing her head.

"Look at everything: the hills and the road and the barns. They'll all be yours pretty soon," Katie told her.

Whisper had a new home.

16

Lake Rollins

"There it is!" said Grandad.

"Gracious!" Gram was craning her neck. "That window's big as a barn door! You'd never have been able to keep it trimmed, let alone wash it."

"I think I'd have managed. But I'm well satisfied where we are," Grandad mildly replied. As they passed what would have been his pharmacy, if he had moved to New Rollins, he drove so slowly that his aging Chevrolet coughed and jerked. "KEN'S AUTOMOTIVE" the sign proclaimed in bold red-and-white letters all across the store front.

"Can we stop a minute?" Katie asked. "I'd like to get out and walk awhile, so I can really look at everything."

"Of course," Grandad instantly replied. "Suppose we go on ahead, and you come to Aunt Harriet's on foot?"

"Perfect!" Katie hopped out and waved.

It was an early morning in April, a day of watery sunshine that didn't warm anything much. Katie had lived in Portland for ten months, except for one wonderful week in late summer, when she had visited Linda on the Rocking C and had ridden Whisper every day: She'd helped Stacey, too; had shown her how Whisper hated to have her halter too tight and loved to nibble fingers with her velvety lips, without hurting a bit; and that she raced best when her rider kept talking to her.

Now Katie walked eagerly along, looking at all the changes. Spindly willows had been planted in rows along Main Street; the doors of Dan's Variety were a blinding red; through the windows of the Golden Quail she could see a brand-new forest of hanging ferns. She darted under the enormous flashing neon sign on the new Sav-U-Mor Drugstore and glanced inside. It was a department store, almost, with aisle after aisle of goods and clattering check-out stands. No wonder Grandad had been afraid of it.

It isn't my Rollins, not any more, Katie thought, moving on again. Instead of shabby little stores, they're all new and shiny, and they all look alike. There's no Bone Creek Ravine, no footbridges. And by tonight it will be stranger still, for it will stand on the shore of a lake, and the hills will seem all stubby and shrunk.

This was the day everyone had waited for, so many years. In just half an hour, at eight o'clock sharp, the gates of the new dam were to be closed. Farther up the Columbia other dams had been storing the spring run-off of melted snow, which they would send downriver in a great surge, to fill the new reservoir in twenty-five hours. By evening the new Lake Rollins would be lapping at the hills, and at nine o'clock tomorrow morning the new dam would open its gates again. Katie, Gram, and Grandad had been up at dawn, to drive from Portland and watch the water come in.

Leaving Main Street, Katie soon found Uncle Steve's house, where a party was already gathered in the back yard. Gram and Grandad were sitting in the shade of a yellow and white beach umbrella, Aunt Harriet was bustling in and out, while Brad, home from college for the day, was supervising an electric grill.

"Sunny side up?" he called when Katie appeared. "Over easy? We aim to please."

"Scrambled, thank you," Katie replied. "When did you come?"

"Last night. Couldn't miss a day like this." He vigorously twirled an egg beater.

Katie could feel her smile growing wider and wider. It was *so* good to see Brad again! "I'm glad you came!" she exclaimed. "It's just like old times."

"Same magnetic guy," he replied, with a grin.

From the sharply sloped back yard Katie had an unbroken view of the river and the site of Old Rollins, where everything had been leveled, right down to the gray pavement of the old streets. Even the pipes had been dug out and basements filled, until the terrain was smooth as a clay bowl. Nothing moved there today. No smoke billowed on the wind. No crash of explosives started rocks to rattling down the hills. Only by counting the asphalt roadways could Katie tell where their store and house had stood.

All of a sudden Allison appeared with her parents in tow. "Isn't it too utterly thrilling?" she said. "By night we'll have a lake! Right here! Almost touching this very town!"

"It's giving me shivers, just thinking about it," Katie agreed. It was coming, it was here—the day they had anticipated so long.

Time slid past, but slowly. All the back yards were crowded, for people from miles around had come to watch the water rise, and Katie could hear subdued talk and laughter. Uncle Steve made pancakes, while Aunt Harriet brought out a heaping bowl of fruit. Allison's mother unpacked a salad and cake, and a few minutes later Linda's family came, her father carrying a box of food and Jeff a basket. Most of it was stowed away in the kitchen, to be served later.

Linda, Katie, and Allison dropped down on the grass together, with the little girls close by. "Whisper's fine," Stacey said with a shy smile.

"Does she still like carrots?" Katie asked.

"Of course," Stacey replied with a giggle. "We have a whole lot in the root cellar, and I feed her some almost every day."

"Good for you."

"Are you coming home with us tonight?" Stacey asked.

"That's right."

"You can ride Whisper tomorrow. I'll ride my pony again. And I'll show you my red ribbon." Stacey and Whisper had placed second at a children's rodeo.

"Thank you." Katie gave the little girl's arm a squeeze. "I'll like that. Allison is coming, too, and we'll have an expedition."

By now the sun was high in the sky. Brad glanced at his watch, peered intently at the river, then jumped to his feet. "Hey! Look, everybody! Spot a marker—that hill, maybe—and watch it. Isn't the water creeping up?"

As Katie stared, the hairs on the back of her neck prickled with excitement. Yes, it was rising already. Bone Creek Ravine seemed wider, fuller, and the shallow apron of bare land, far down by the river—surely it hadn't been so narrow before.

Now the group settled down for a long day,

adults in chairs under the umbrellas, students sprawled on the grass a little farther down the slope. The first excitement was replaced by melancholy, a sense of time and change and the passing of old ways.

"If I watch the water—hard," Katie said, "it doesn't seem to rise. But if I look at a certain rock, like that yellow one right at the edge, and look away for a few minutes, and then look back—the rock is gone."

"Sure," said Brad. "It's rising all right. And it will come faster when water from the farthest dams gets here."

It became a game. There's a rock—look away—and back—and it's vanished.

Everyone fell silent, for the jagged slit of Bone Creek Ravine was almost filled. It's at Old Rollins now, thought Katie. This is the saddest part of all.

The gully overflowed. A watery shine crept along the site of old Main Street. The place where Dan's Variety had stood was covered . . . the Golden Quail . . . Sanders Hardware. Already it seemed like a lake, wider than before, and the hills not quite so high.

"It's at Grandad's store," breathed Katie, thinking of the Last Day of Business, and how everyone had stood weeping in the street, while the siren blew.

"Look at it come!" shouted someone in a nearby yard. Farther away a boy's voice chanted a few lines of "Ol' Man River," but no one joined in, and the boy soon stopped. This was not a day for singing.

Water rose against the bluff, against the hills. "Stone Canyon's all shiny," said Allison, with a catch in her voice. "Katie, remember the day you broke your ankle?"

"Could I ever forget?"

Still the water rose.

"There's the Congregational Church," said Katie. And later, "The old school—oh, Allison!" She choked. "There it is in our street! I can see waves already, lapping where our yards used to be. Over Grandad's garden. Remember when we met there?"

"The night we rescued Chrys? And he's turned into such a big cat. He's even quit climbing trees."

The water was rising fast now, and a brisk wind was tossing its surface into iridescent splinters of gray and blue, silver and black. The old town was covered, but New Rollins was still a long way above the growing lake, and there were hours to go.

Toward evening Uncle Steve lighted the barbecue and began to grill hamburgers, while the picnic baskets were emptied and food set out.

"I'm stuffed," said Allison, later on.

"A couple more burgers here, going to waste!" Brad called out. "Jeff?"

"Not me." Jeff groaned and stretched out on the ground.

And still the flood crept higher. "I can't believe it! The lake is getting so wide!" Katie exclaimed, half under her breath. She hadn't known there was this much water anywhere, except in the ocean.

"And by tomorrow it'll be wider still," Uncle Steve said.

As a breeze began to toss whitecaps on the growing lake, the boys talked football, and the girls compared notes about school. Linda told them the play *Finian's Rainbow* was soon to be given.

"After all my dreams about footlights," she wryly said, "about having fans, and signing autographs . . . look at this." She held out her hand, showing a purple fingernail. "Hammered it, helping build a set. I've learned one thing. Freshmen are expendable."

Katie laughed. "I've got marks, too, only mine are harder to show." She proudly pulled her jeans above a large black-and-blue spot on her leg, with a scab in the center. "There's a worse one, higher up. From gymnastics. I was practicing a cast tuck on the high bar."

"Sounds tricky."

"It's tricky, all right. But fun. The class is over before I know it, and I practice almost every day after school with the freshman team. At least this is one place where it pays to be small. There's not so much of me to flip around."

"So we both have honorable wounds," Linda said. "What else have you been doing?"

"Missing Rollins," Katie began, "But—" She was

struck by a sudden thought. "But I'm so rushed that a day is gone before it's begun."

"I know," Allison agreed. "I never have half enough time. Do you like your classes?"

"Well—some are fine, some only so-so. One is a real pain. But my lit teacher is super." Katie paused, thinking about Mr. Henderson, and about Cheryl Kessler, who sat beside her in his class and lived just down the street. She and Cheryl had had some good times working out the assignments. What was it Gram had told her once? *You'll always have friends*. She had Cheryl already, and Maureen Hyatt in Spanish class, and Janie Peterson. And Greg Logan, with his touseled hair and broad grin, who sat at her table in science lab. She and Greg worked experiments together pretty often.

"Are you singing?" Linda asked.

"In the freshman chorus. We did *The Messiah* at Christmas, with massed choirs from all over the city and the junior symphony." Katie stopped again, remembering the thundering bass of the orchestra, the chant of the organ. "It was really super!" she said, and looked up to find Aunt Harriet beside her with a plate of cookies. As her aunt smiled and nodded, ever so slightly, Katie almost seemed to hear again what she had said, that long-ago day. *You'll be all right. You're a survivor*.

That's true! Katie thought, in a sudden, wild,

jumbled flash of understanding. *I am all right! In fact, I'm just fine! I'm still me—and nothing can change that.*

"We did three performances in the city auditorium," she finished with a rush of pride. She'd had Whisper, the ranch, the rodeo, and nothing could take them away. They'd be part of her, forever. She'd always love Whisper, and maybe she'd have another horse someday. But right now she was happy doing something else.

By dusk, all the colored marks on the bluff were covered, although the water still had many feet to rise. It had now come so close that the watchers could hear the splash of waves on the shore. Sunset red shone in every ripple, along with darkening silver and great shadowed depths, far out. A lonely duck winged past, black against the glow.

As the sky darkened, a star appeared, the breeze dropped, and everything was still. On the hills of the new town a light came on, and another, and another. Far away, incredibly far, shone a glimmer on the opposite shore.

"The old town is gone, truly gone," Katie said. "It's been destroyed three times. By crushing. By fire. By water. There's nothing left of it, anywhere on earth."

She stood up. The day was over, just as the old life was over. Now the new life would go on. Tonight she would spend with Linda at the Rocking C. In the morning she would have a long, glorious ride on Whisper, with Linda and Allison and the little sisters, too.

But after the ride she would drive back to the city with Gram and Grandad. She would work out with the gymnastics team again and learn some harder routines. She would return to the chorus, to Cheryl and Janie. To science lab. To her yellow-and-white room.

Tomorrow she would be going home.

Author's Note

The town of Rollins exists only in imagination, along with all the people in it. Neither Katie, nor her grandparents, nor her friends, lived anywhere along any river.

However, people in all sections of the country know what it is like to live in a town that has to be moved. On the Columbia River system alone more than two hundred dams have been erected, and countless others have been constructed elsewhere. Some of these have displaced farms—or homes—or entire towns. The building is still going on. The town of North Bonneville, Washington, has recently been relocated because the height of Bonneville Dam was increased, and new dams are constantly being planned in other parts of the nation.

Even though this story is fiction, the details of picking up a town and setting it down in another place are basically true. I have visited Arlington in Oregon and Roosevelt in Washington, both of which were moved because of the John Day Dam on the Columbia River. People who lived in these towns told me what it was like: the explosions, the dust, the shoo-fly railroad, and the Last Day of Business. These are things that really happened.

The lake behind the John Day Dam, which is most like the one in this book, was to have been filled in twenty-five hours, a day and a night. However, that evening, when the water had reached half its final height, a leak in a railroad embankment was found, which required a pause of several days. Even so, the first part of the filling had proceeded on schedule. Anyone who was there could have watched the water come in, just as Katie does in the book.

The washout of the bridge is also founded on fact. While the John Day Dam was being built, a new highway bridge was erected across the John Day River, just above its junction with the Columbia. Bedrock under the river was so difficult to reach that the middle pier of the bridge was set on compacted sand and gravel instead. Just before Christmas, 1964, during a severe flood, that pier gave way, causing the center of the bridge to collapse. In this case, no Katie sounded the alarm. Two cars were on the bridge when it happened, and one man plunged to his death, although the other people managed to make it back to solid ground.

I would like to thank several residents of Arlington and Roosevelt who gave me the picture of moving a town. These include Mr. and Mrs. Marion T. Weatherford, Mrs. Ben Crippen, Mr. Foster Odom, and Diane Clough, all of whom were most friendly and helpful. Meeting people like these is one of the rewards of being a writer.

DOROTHY NAFUS MORRISON